MURDER AT STONE'S THROW

MURDER AT STONE'S THROW

A novel

Peggy Baseman

iUniverse, Inc.

New York Lincoln Shanghai

MURDER AT STONE'S THROW

iUniverse books may be ordered through booksellers or by contacting:

iUniverse
2021 Pine Lake Road, Suite 100
Lincoln, NE 68512
www.iuniverse.com
1-800-Authors (1-800-288-4677)

Because of the dynamic nature of the Internet, any Web addresses or links contained in this book may have changed since publication and may no longer be valid.

This is a work of fiction. All of the characters, names, incidents, organizations, and dialogue in this novel are either the products of the author's imagination or are used fictitiously.

ISBN: 978-0-595-46981-9 (pbk)
ISBN: 978-0-595-91265-0 (ebk)

Printed in the United States of America

CHAPTER 1

▼

Acumulada del Rio Maria Candelario sensed snow in the air. Her gold front teeth, the proud handiwork of Dr. Leandro Maria Jesus Fernandez, the number one (and only) dentist of Lindo Labio, San Salvador, ached in that familiar way. Her dental weather predictions were rarely wrong. When it was particularly cold, the pain was sharp and piercing; rain was forecast by a dull throb. But, when snow was coming, the throb became jungle drums, hundreds of them, beating up through her cheekbones to her right eyeball. The drums were making serious music now. Snow was on the way, of that there was no doubt. Acumulada had not consulted Dr. Fernandez regarding the odd meteorological powers with which her dental work had endowed her. In the tropical climes of Lindo Labio, snow and piercing cold detection were usually not topics of general conversation. Even if Lindo Labio had been located at a higher latitude, a conversation with her dentist would not have taken place. In fact, Acumulada had never again had a conversation with or even seen Dr. Leandro Maria Jesus Fernandez and had never again visited Lindo Labio. On that January day in 1969 just as soon as the cement had dried on her golden weather predictors, Acumulada rinsed, spit, rose from the dentist's chair and walked the two streets over to her brother Miguel's house. There, she collected the two cardboard boxes that she'd received from America, the cardboard boxes which, with a slight rearrangement of the contents were to become her luggage. She kissed Miguel goodbye and boarded the donkey cart for the drive to Gastado Chacharro. In Gastado Chacharro, she would catch the tap tap bus for the seven-hour trip to el Salvador where she would board a plane for San Juan. From San Juan, she would fly to Miami and from Miami to

Boston to be met by her new employer. From that day forward, Lindo Labio was nothing more than a dim, dusty, donkey filled memory.

Marla Babcock Saltonstall Stone leaned forward and took a light from her father's Zippo.

"Didn't you just put one out?" Lorraine Babcock Saltonstall did not approve of young ladies smoking and, particularly did not approve of her own daughter engaging in the filthy habit. Lorraine, of course, smoked herself, but that was an entirely different matter. She'd smoked for years, just one or two now and then, yes, just one or two now and then, and she smoked menthols. It was entirely different. And, for the boys it was one thing, but not for a young lady. Marla had not learned to smoke from her mother. Smoking was just one of the little habits her daughter had picked up during the year she had spent in London after graduating from Barnard. Smoking and the use of obscure Britishisms which crept unexpectedly into her speech, especially during stressful moments. Like this one.

"Oh, Mum. If I don't have a fag, I'll eat something and I positively can't have another digestive. I think I've put on a stone."

"Really, Marla. I'm surprised Ledge doesn't object."

"To what?"

Leland Edgar Stone, "Ledge" since the second day of his life, did not object at all. In fact, he had so little interest in anything Marla did, he was perhaps unaware of his young bride's addiction to tobacco or her odd linguistic choices. Ledge spent his days and many of his nights totally immersed in the affairs of the affluent widows and orphans whose substantial assets he helped to manage at the Federal Asset Retention Trust. So enamoured were FART's clients of their charming young administrator that they showed no shame fawning over him, competing with one another for his attention. These women had reached the age where they no longer needed to show discretion in their admiration of a hand-some, well-built, virile, somewhat slow-witted young man with perfect teeth. Ledge lapped it up. He couldn't get enough of his corseted, eye-lifted, clientele. By the time he returned home at the end of a long day, Ledge's capacity for human interaction had been entirely spent. He gave nothing to and asked noth-ing of Marla other than the performance of her conjugal duty on a somewhat reg-ular basis. The best parts of Ledge's personality were stored in the vest pocket of his chalk stripe suit. Once that vest was hanging in the closet, he might just as well have been a cardboard cutout.

"Daddy, make her stop."

"Lorraine, dear, leave the girl alone." Her father inhaled deeply on his Camel. Waldo Saltonstall's gaze drifted across the tarmac. He loved airports; he loved airplanes; he loved aviation. He would have been a flyer if his vision had been good enough. He would have joined the Army Air Corps. He would have served his country in the big war. He'd had responsibilities though. His family's paper business was not going to run itself if he'd just up and enlisted. He'd done his part in the war effort. Armies may match on their stomachs, but they had other needs as well. Armies as well as civilians needed rolled tissue and boxed facial and he'd provided it. He'd done his part. But, aviation. That was the future. He would have loved to have flown. He would have loved to have had his future up in the clouds, but it just wasn't meant to be. He traveled by air whenever he could, but it wasn't the same. How he longed to just one time have the experience of sitting up there in the cockpit, headphones and aviator sunglasses in place and give that thumbs up to the ground crew. But, it just wasn't meant to be. He had never even sat in the copilot's seat. Never been invited. No one he knew was an aviator; no one he knew was in a position to invite him up for a barnstorming spin. There was that Holmes character with the helicopter. But, if he had ever approached him, ever tried to invite himself for a ride, Lorraine would have had a fit. Planes were one thing; helicopters quite another. If the truth be told, no one in his social strata was even aware of his fascination with aviation. As far as everyone in his social circle knew, he had no interests other than business. He was a paper man. He made tissue, he sold tissue, he provided for his family. Ah, but to fly …

"Shouldn't this plane have arrived by now?" Marla's irritated tone jolted her father from his cloud hopping reverie. Patience was not one of Marla's particular strengths on a good day. On a day when she had the pleasure of her mother's company for several uninterrupted hours, patience was not even a possibility.

Waldo consulted his watch. The flight was not scheduled to arrive for another fifteen minutes. As usual, his daughter showed none of the quiet patience that had been his stock in trade.

The Saltonstalls had picked Marla up in Brookline and driven along Storrow Drive to the airport to meet this senorita about whom she had been so keen. Setting up housekeeping was difficult enough for a pair of newlyweds, but, without the proper help, it could become a nightmare. Marla, headstrong as usual, refused her mother's offer of a nice Irish girl. Margaret McDonough had been with the Saltonstall family for years and she had sisters, cousins, nieces and friends galore, all of whom would give their eyeteeth (if any of them still had them) to move in and keep house for a young and, as yet childless couple in a spacious Brookline apartment. But, no. Marla had insisted on hiring a young woman from Latin

America, a woman she could train herself, a woman who would owe no debt to her mother, the formidable Lorraine Babcock Saltonstall. Lorraine Babcock Saltonstall did not care for situations which did not include at least a modicum of indebtedness to her and whenever it was at all possible, saw to it that at least *someone* felt they owed her *something*.

At last flight 1284 from Miami was announced. At least Marla prayed the undecipherable gibberish being broadcast through the airport PA system was flight 1284 from Miami. Mother, father and only child huddled by the window, pulling cashmere sweaters, Harris tweeds and mink stoles tighter around their shoulders to protect themselves from the sight of the cold. They peered out to the runway. Six little oval frosts of breath from three Patrician noses steamed the glass which separated the comfortably heated VIP lounge from the bone chilling gusts of the January afternoon. The stairs were rolled over as the plane's door opened and passengers began to disembark. No. No. Not that one. No. Oh, my God. That must be her. Lorraine's old hot pink Jackie Kennedy boucle suit (complete with pillbox hat) appeared at the top of the stairs. It might as well have been Dallas in 1963, but for the fact that the suit was at least two sizes too big for the scrawny frame of the ill fed Acumulada del Rio Maria Candelario. Over the shoulders of the tiny Latina was draped a once tres chic three-quarter length beaver. The beaver Marla recognized as having belonged to her grandmother, the late Ethel Lowell Babcock. From where she stood, the coat didn't look half bad. Marla was a little miffed that her mother hadn't offered it to her, but instead had mailed it off to Acumulada in Lindo Labio along with the boucle suit and God only knew what else without ever having mentioned a word to Marla. As Acumulada started down the stairs, she squinted into the harsh setting sun and searched for who knows what in the direction of the terminal building. Her lips parted as her head turned, exposing the flashing smile which was to become her trademark. The smile quickly turned to a frown then a grimace. The precious metal mouth, the result of the combination of Dr. Leandro Maria Jesus Fernandez's handiwork and, as it would later be revealed, Lorraine Babcock Saltonstall's dineros were, for the first time, exposed to the climate of the Northern Hemisphere and, for the first time, telegraphed their throbbing weather forecast.

Marla silently cursed her poor planning. She should have been the one to have sent clothes to Acumulada; she should have been the one to have sent her money for dental work. But, she didn't know. How could she have known? How did Lorraine Babcock Saltonstall know? On that January day, in that VIP lounge, with her father's Camel depositing its yellow nicotine stain on her manicured fingers, she made a vow.

"Never again. As God is my witness, never again will I let poor planning and lack of foresight put me in a position where Mother or anyone else has the upper hand on Marla Saltonstall Stone."

CHAPTER 2

▼

The snow was definitely coming. Although Acumulada had been in the States for over 30 years, she had not become accustomed to that *muy frio* that came over her every winter. In the old days, Missus Marla would move everybody down to the house on Brazilian Avenue right after Christmas. Family services at The First Unitarian Church, ooh and aah over the fountain pens and cashmere sweaters that everyone seemed to give one another every year, then pack up golf clothes and bathing suits and fly to Palm Beach until Easter. The linchpins of the Christian calendar served to bookmark the family's annual north/south migration. Acumulada managed to dash into St. Edward's when she could, but knew God would understand if most of her prayers originated from whichever kitchen she was manning during each liturgical period.

Once they were settled in Palm Beach, the boys, - Marla's and Acumulada's - had no trouble adjusting to the new routine of tutors in the morning and golf, tennis and riding coaches in the afternoon. The Essex School saw no difficulty in this schedule. In fact, so many of the boys were away for the winters in various moderate climates, that several of Essex's faculty members were assigned the task of creating a sort of correspondence course – a curriculum which the Florida tutors followed. After Easter, when the boys returned, they sat for the examinations with the rest of the students. Billy and Charlie usually passed. Fernando and Carlos Candelario headed the class.

Marla and Ledge had, since childhood, taken this respite from the cold New England weather; they needed this break from the winter. But, unlike many of their circle who sent the children off to board at the earliest possible date, they didn't want to be separated from their boys for such a long stretch. And, they absolutely positively couldn't bear to be away from Acumulada for any period of time. So, bag and baggage, the whole troop – Marla's boys, Acumulada's boys and Ledge, the ultimate (perpetual) boy – flew south for the winter. Lolly and Waldo always arrived the day after Marla and her family. They never would be on the same flight lest the loss of both generations of the family in the fiery wreckage of a downed plane would confuse the estate and trust managers beyond all hope. Lolly and Waldo had long ago given their house to Marla and Ledge and spent their winter in a bungalow on the grounds of The Breakers.

The Palm Beach parties, most of which were held in the ballroom of The Breakers, were very important for Ledge's business. Most of his clients at FART spent the winter down south and it was important that he be available to them. Marla attended these parties and played tennis and sailed and entertained and smiled and was charming to the women who hated her guts for having landed the much sought after Ledge. She of course, was always the perfect wife, but that was not enough for her. During those winters, when she could break away from visits with her parents, much of her time was spent researching and experimenting with ethnic or vegetarian cooking, trying new gardening techniques (indoors and out) or mastering the art of flowering arranging. These were things she loved and things she was good at. These were things she preferred over perfecting her back-hand. In a particularly heated conversation about the way she spent what little free time she had, Ledge made it very clear that he thought she was an idiot. It was not too long before Marla realized that the feeling was mutual.

CHAPTER 3

▼

Snow. Missus Marla was not going to be happy. This season's snow plowing budget had been blown by December and it was still coming down in March. Guido Benedetto was a nice guy and just about the only one of the legions of local gardener/snow plowers who would even come across the rickety bridge to take care of that cobblestone driveway. There was just too much hand shoveling and the customer too demanding for most of the others to even consider doing it for any amount of money. Guido was a nice guy, but he wasn't a stupid guy. He put up with her, charged her top dollar and she had to pay it. Acumulada's not inconsiderable Latina charms were much admired by Guido, but these charms had been powerless against Guido's exorbitant hourly rate.

During the gardening season, Marla had been able to keep Guido's bills down by doing a lot of the routine work herself. With the obvious exception of mowing the two plus acres of formal lawn on the property and shearing the eight-foot privet hedge, there were quite a few chores she could do herself. Herself, of course, with the help of the very well trained Acumulada. Although she'd never had more than a tiny chicken scratched dirt patch back home in Lindo Labio, Acumulada showed a remarkable aptitude for precise and complicated horticulture and she assumed full responsibility for many areas of the 9 acre island. Nevertheless, Guido was needed every day for at least a few hours and drove across the tiny, rickety old bridge back and forth from Stone's Throw at least ten times per week.

Marla had never been a slug-a-bed. But, in the years since Ledge had left her for Florence Bainbridge, Marla's sleep requirement had become less and less. In fact, by now, she functioned quite well on about four hours per night and that was decreasing all the time. In fact, her nightly four hours produced a level of competence that far exceeded that of many eight-hour sleepers she knew. Thus, was she able to teach her food styling and presentation class on Tuesday, her gold leafing and stenciling class on Thursday, her cooking class on Monday, her Chinese herbal remedy class on Wednesday, her four season gardening and introduction to birdsong class on Saturday morning and her periodic jam and jelly workshops and still have time to run her own life (with the help of Acumulada). She continued to write her monthly home and garden newsletter during her copious free time. The newsletter started as a little blurb she'd send out to friends and neighbors just for her own fun. The recipients loved it so much she expanded her mailing list and began charging for it. Needless to say, she'd absolutely die before she'd ever keep a nickel of the proceeds. That would not have been right. Everything went to the Society for Homeless in Transition. It was one of her favorite causes. Over the course of its somewhat brief history, it had helped so many. Daddy had established it back in the days when he could do such things and there was no way she would let this last vestige of his generosity disappear. Her classes were quite another story. She charged for them and people paid and paid willingly. They were, in fact, lining up to pay. There was a waiting list for every one of Marla's classes. It gave her a good feeling to know people at last respected what she was doing.

All of the classes were held in the 24 room French Normandy house, Stone's Throw, which, along with a guest house, stables, cabanas and various outbuildings, sat on the 9 acre island, the free and clear title to which Marla had received in the divorce settlement. The free and clear title to Stone's Throw was pretty much the only thing Marla had gotten in the settlement.

Marla's class participants crossed the charming rustic bridge and used the cobblestone driveway to park and to walk across to the front door. The stones were pink jumbos, approximately two pieces per square foot, 68 pieces per ton. There was no question that the driveway cobblestones were lovely. There was no question that they were a snow plowing nightmare. There could be not one errant flake, not one icy cobble, not one slimy wet moss patch on the driveway. Not while Marla still had breath in her body. There would be not one opportunity for some sleazy personal injury lawyer to relieve her of her last few dollars because of a "slip and fall". Of course, Marla carried liability insurance, but she'd be damned if poor planning and lack of foresight forced her to make an unnecessary claim and up her premiums. Her clients (she never called them students) would walk safely and uneventfully from their vehicles to her front door because Guido was paid to see to it that they could.

And, now more. More snow. Again. Poor missus. Poor Missus Marla. Guido would have to come. He'd have to plow; he'd have to shovel; he'd have to sprinkle kitty litter (residual rock salt tracked into the house was much too harsh on the Orientals and the parquet) and he'd have to send a hefty bill. Guido was a nice guy, but he had to make a living too.

Acumulada licked her front teeth. Maybe she felt a little throb starting. Maybe this snow would change to rain. Rain doesn't have to be plowed. Rain just dries. Maybe. Por favor. Por favor. She made the sign of the cross and bowed her head in silent prayer.

Guido was no longer a young man, but neither was Acumulada a young woman. Fortunata had passed on ten years earlier after having borne and raised Guido's eleven children. Acumulada had never married, never legally. For 30 years, Ramon came and went. He was in prison; he was out. He was in the old country; he was back. He was married to his first wife; he was widowed. Ramon was a lot of work. For a man who claimed to be descended from Spanish royalty, he could not have been less regal. Her boys, though - those boys. Regal bearing must skip generations. No one could be more regal than her Carlos and Fernando. And, mercifully, they had been spared Ramon's jug ears. But, when all was said and done, her relationship with their father was a fine one from Acumulada's point of view. It suited her. She did not have a great deal of time to devote to a "relationship". Her first priority, after all was Missus Marla. Missus Marla needed her in many, many ways and there usually was not time for a guy like Ramon. After she'd had Carlos and Fernando, as far as she was concerned, Ramon's usefulness was over.

As the years passed, though, with her children grown, she began to long for the companionship only a man could provide. Guido fit the bill. He had his own life and his own family. He had his own friends and his softball team mates. She didn't have to wash his socks; didn't have to deal with his children or his sainted mother. And, he lived in town, well on the other side of the worn and frankly, somewhat dangerous, bridge which he crossed at the end of each day to return to his real life, his life with his nightly dinner prepared just so by his spinster daughter, Gina; his Wednesday night pinochle game; his weekly bets on every horse race between here and Siciliy and Sunday dinner with Angelina and the grandchildren. Guido had a full and happy life. But, when he was on her side of the bridge, now, that was another matter. After all, how long does companionship take? Acumulada experienced Guido's companionship in the tool shed, down in the wine cellar and, in the warm weather behind the privet hedge. In some ways, it was too bad that Missus Marla had to cut Guido's hours. What she didn't realize was that she was cutting seriously into Acumulada's social life. Guido was a faithful man. In the ten years since Fortunata had passed, he'd never even thought of another woman. Fortunata had devoted her life to Guido and their eleven children, one of whom still lived at home to care for her father. Her memory was as precious to him as she had been in her lifetime. He never even thought of another woman. Except, of course, for Acumulada del Rio Maria Candelario. She was different, special, magical. Her smile, her laugh, her cooking.

✳   ✳   ✳   ✳

ACUMULADA'S SALVADOREAN SHRIMP

¼ cup olive oil	2 cloves garlic, chopped
1 onion sliced	1 green pepper, chopped
2 tsps. Tabasco	1 large tomato, chopped
2 Tbsps. Tomato paste	2/3 cup coconut milk
1 tsp. Cilantro	juice of 2 lemons
¼ cup sesame oil	1 lb. shrimp, peeled and deveined

Saute onion and garlic in oil until translucent. Add green pepper, tomatoes, tomato paste and tabasco. Cook until vegetables are tender. Add coconut milk, cilantro, lemon juice and sesame oil. Cook additional five minutes on low heat. Add shrimp and cook until shrimp turns pink. Serve over rice.

Things had been easier when Ledge had been alive. With those alimony checks coming in like clockwork every month, Marla could afford to keep up the house the way it should be kept up. She could afford her massage therapist. She could afford her $300 jars of face creams. She could afford her specifically prescribed Chinese herbal teas prepared monthly for her by Mr. Woo. She could afford to keep her chi on an even keel. Ledge Stone had had some advantages. More specifically, Ledge Stone's alimony had some advantages.

All four boys were now grown up. Charles and Billy were playing lacrosse at Amherst College. Her handsome boys were across the road at the University of Massachusetts. Thank God for old Mr. Saltonstall, may he rest in peace. He'd set aside money for his grandsons' education when they were infants. He'd generously thrown in a few extra bucks earmarked for Carlos and Fernando. It's a good thing he did it when he did. He never could have predicted how things would turn out for him. He never could have imagined how he'd lose everything – the paper mill, his houses, his investments – in order to pay off his former employees who claimed the chemicals he used in the manufacture of his paper had damaged their health. These were the same employees Mr. Saltonstall had cared for, fought for and supported for as long as anyone could remember. These were the sons and grandsons of mill workers his father before him had supported. But, suddenly, the chemicals they'd always used had become "toxic". Suddenly, there could be a payday. They could make health claims and someone would have to pay. Someone with deep pockets. That someone was Waldo Saltonstall. He'd paid. He'd paid with every dime he had and then he paid some more. He'd blown his brains out in the basement of his Brookline office. Charles and Billy never knew their grandfather.

Life had been blissfully quiet for a few years. The boys were thriving; Marla was happy teaching a class here and there and writing her monthly newsletter. The constant squabbling which defined the early years had ended when Ledge had moved out and Ramon had dropped out of sight. Ramon had either returned to his wife or had been nailed for an unpaid gambling debt. Acumulada never knew exactly what had happened to him. Whatever it was, it didn't happen with her. All she knew was that things were quiet. It was during those quiet years that Acumulada had begun to appreciate the charms of Guido, a quiet man, a man of few words. He was the perfect man for those quiet years. His eyes were quiet, his rough callused hands were quiet, the little unlit cigars clenched between his teeth were quiet. The only things about Guido that were not quiet were his lawn mower and snowplow.

For a long time, Acumulada had looked forward to that familiar zinging in her facial sinuses. She looked forward to snow. It meant Guido would be coming. His winter visits were less regular than during mowing season. Their eyes would meet. They'd spend a stolen minute here, a stolen minute there. Once their relationship had been established, though, once they had become accustomed to spending time together in the tool shed, in the wine cellar, and in the good weather, behind the privet hedge, her thrilling snow anticipation lost its luster. Then, her snow sensing teeth became what they'd actually always been –annoying curiosities. Annoying curiosities that predicted that Guido would be away from her, off servicing his other customers. Well, at least plowing other driveways.

The quiet years didn't last. How could they? Acumulada del Rio Maria Candelario was never meant to live a quiet life. Her early years living by her wits in the streets and alleys of Lindo Labio did not prepare her for a life of quiet non-events, had not prepared her for years of vacuuming and putting up jam and trimming topiaries on a tiny island that plate techtonics had snapped off the Massachusetts coast. And, Marla Babcock Saltonstall Stone was certainly never destined to live a quiet life.

With the alimony checks coming in like clockwork every month, the quiet was easily maintained. But, once Ledge's body was found stuffed into the surprisingly spacious trunk of Florence Bainbridge's Bentley, everything changed. Dead men tell no tales. The investigation never came up with anything definitive. It was common knowledge that Scott Bainbridge was positively mortified by the idea of his mother openly carrying on with Ledge Stone. Ledge had been his classmate at Yale, for gods sake. But, no one could make any connection between Scott and the murder. He had an airtight alibi. He was trekking through the Himalayas somewhere between Tibet and Nepal when Ledge met his untimely end. Scott's underworld connections were widely hinted at, but, no one could ever prove anything, so Stone's death was eventually classified as a "cold case" but, as far as the members of The Club were concerned, Scott Bainbridge got away with murder.

Dead men tell no tales. Dead men also pay no alimony. Ledge was never one to put anything away for a rainy day, especially if the only one likely to be dampened by that rainy day was his ex-wife. Ledge had effectively squandered anything he had been left by his family and was living from hand to mouth, just squeaking by with barely enough to make Marla's monthly alimony. His lifestyle continued to be comfortable to say the least, thanks to the generosity of good old Florence. But, on his own, Ledge's personal D & B was not a pretty sight. So, once Ledge was history, so was Marla's income.

CHAPTER 4

▼

Marla inhaled deeply. The pungent smell of the fresh ginger root she was adding to the boiling water was almost enough to center her chi. Almost, but not quite. Mr. Woo had prescribed a new tea for her - something to calm her jangled nerves. He'd felt her pulses and had declared her blood far too hot. He recommended she let some of her worry escape. Perhaps chanting - permitting sound to escape from her body and accompanying herself on a drum while she drank her tea would help her relax. The loud banging and chant would carry her worries far off into another dimension. This could, should, according to Mr. Woo, cool her blood. She'd boiled up the odd assortment of dried mushrooms, stems, leaves, bark and what looked New England topsoil and was just adding the one and only ingredient she could purchase at the local Stop & Shop. Usually, his teas did the trick, especially if they were taken in conjunction with meditation and visualization. This time, though, it just didn't seem to be happening despite the three days of the nauseating stuff for breakfast, lunch and dinner along with a percussion accompaniment. She was broke, that was all there was to it. All the banging, chanting and herbal tea in the world were not going to change that. She needed money and had no idea how to go about getting it. Her bills were skyrocketing and there was just no money to pay them. She'd deferred home maintenance too long. The cobblestone driveway needed to be redone. The slate roof and copper valleys and down spouts could no longer just be patched, the complete roof had to be replaced. The chintz slipcovers were fading; the silk ones oxidizing; the sheer window panels were disintegrating right there where they hung. The pool needed to be retiled; there hadn't been goldfish in the pond for two years; the parquet floors needed to be refinished; the brick needed to be repointed; the boiler leaked and the central air conditioning system hadn't worked for three summers. The house was falling down around her ears and now here was a tax bill. What nerve! Who the hell did those people think they were? After all she'd done for this town, never asking a thing in return, never even using the schools, the fire department, the trash pick up. Heck, she'd plowed and maintained her own roads and bridges. She should just secede from the town of Hammerston. And she could do it. Just declare her little island an independent political entity. Heck, why not an independent country. At most, she voted in Hammerston and drove her car through there on their pathetic ill maintained roads on her way to Boston or somewhere else. Who did they think they were, sending this kind of tax bill? She'd have to seek an abatement. Of course, she had no idea how to go about doing that. All she could think of was to call Young, Young & Silverberg and ask them to take care of it. Of course, no one at Young, Young & Silverberg worked for free. Those snakes didn't say good morning to their wives without billing. Old Mr. Young might be willing to help her out, but, these days he was little more than a doddering old codger who came in to have his morning coffee, use the postage meter and take an afternoon nap. He had so little power now and, frankly, so little memory, that for sure she'd be handed off to one of the other lawyers. The fact that her family's personal interests and her father's paper mill had essentially created the now highly regarded law firm was conveniently forgotten by young Mr. Young and his partners. All they cared about was the number of hours they could bill. They didn't answer the phone without noting the number of six-minute increments they'd spent. A tenth of an hour was a tenth of an hour and they owed it to their partners never to give away what they could bill for. Young, Young & Silverberg was not the answer. What Marla needed was more money, not more bills.

Goddamn Ledge. Her father had always said he was worth more dead than alive. That was, of course, before the divorce, before he cashed in every one of his insurance policies. People said it was to pay off gambling debts. Marla knew better. Ledge may have enjoyed a friendly game now and then, but he was not addicted to gambling. What he was addicted to was gratitude. He loved giving money away. He loved the gratitude of those to whom he gave it. He loved being fawned over as he boyishly shrugged that "aw shucks, it was nuthin'" shrug. He was glad just to be able to help. He did good, worthwhile things with it. While his own sons were supported by their grandfather's foresight, he supported the children of his office staff through medical school. Only medical school. He refused, on general principle with which Marla could not disagree, to pay for law school. He financed an inner city performing arts center that was named in his honor. He assumed the role of patron of a local artist with a somewhat narrow following. Lulu Noone's signature style was totally blank canvasses trimmed in neon tubing. He owned hundreds. Each one was identical, identical except for the placement and color of the tubing. To be fair, the paintings weren't just blank canvasses. They began, as all paintings do, as white canvasses. Upon these white canvasses, Ms. Noone spent weeks painting delicately shaded bowls of ripe nectarines in one corner, a sad clown portrait in another, kittens napping in a wicker basket in another. These works would then be vigorously and totally covered with gobs and blobs of what seemed to be random colors and abstract images until not one bit of the still life or kittens or country lane was visible. Next, a layer of finely ground glass, found objects and bits of organic material, soil, cat hair, and dryer lint was applied, building up a thick, irregular, almost lumpy surface. Locked in her coldwater flat with her two unusually large and vocal cats, Stock and Barrel, (Lock, unfortunately had not been blessed with nine lives) she would crank up her stereo and listen to ancient LP's of The Ventures and Connie Francis. Her paintings reflected the ambient sound and were either rhythmically rocking or plaintively whiny. After a week or so, when the paint had dried and the cat hair and other three dimensional particles had admixed sufficiently, the records would be changed to something like Mantovanni or 101 Strings. Only LP's, never CD's or any music more recent than 1973. With her little mind worked into her version of angst, she'd get out the power sprayer and work furiously to cover in white house paint the lasagnes she'd created, envisioning the exact and optimal location of the colored neon tubing which was the finishing touch. Lulu Noone's work had had some critical success. It was just enough to convince her and her one and only patron that she should continue working, and continue working in her own unique style. She produced a remarkable number of these works. Most of them were sitting in a closet in Marla's basement, having been purchased by the ever generous Ledge. He had reserved for himself a few walls in the house on which to hang a selection of his collection. Two walls in the dining room and all four walls in what was his home office displayed an ever changing, expensively lighted Noone show. While Lulu Noone was still around and still flinging paint (and God only knew what else) against canvasses, there was no way any of these creations would represent anything more than dust collectors. Now, if Ms. Noone were to join the unfortunate late little Lock in cat and cat lover's heaven …

Every dime Ledge had inherited he had spent. His salary at FART was a mere pittance relative to the amounts he was throwing around. The kids he'd supported through medical school had since become dermatologists and ophthalmologists and had forgotten all about their wealthy patron until one of them needed to buy a new laser to start a skin resurfacing practice and tried to hit him up for the seed money. The performing arts center never attracted the names he'd anticipated. The best it had ever done was a Dodie Goodman poetry reading and a book signing by Donna Reed's biographer. And Noone. Although her lifestyle was far from luxurious, Lulu Noone consumed a fair amount of non-tax-deductible cash every month. That old buzzard was still alive and kicking, still covering her still lifes with cat hair and white paint and obsessing over where the neon tubing should be placed. Suffice it to say that Ledge's philanthropies had not worked out as he'd expected. When he was alive, Marla could at least nag him for his alimony payments. And, when it became absolutely necessary, she could turn to her father. But, who could have imagined that Waldo's money would ever run out? Who could have imagined that Waldo's life would ever run out? But, it had and all Marla's resources had run dry.

She sipped her tea and banged on a goatskin drum while chanting the mantra Mr. Woo had created for her. "RRRR". She tried to visualize her troubles and worries and problems circulating through her body. She willed them out of her mouth via each drumbeat-accompanied grunt. "RRRR". She blew and grunted, blew and grunted. Something wasn't working. It just wasn't working. It usually helped, but this time, it just wasn't working.

She could call Mr. Woo and ask him for a different preparation, but another preparation would mean another charge on her Visa. She'd promised herself that her American Express platinum card was to be used only for the most dire emergencies. Did this qualify? She couldn't bear the shame she would feel if her herbalist's charge were declined because her credit card had maxed out.

There had to be a way. She could always get a job selling shoes at Saks. But, then again, probably not. She had far too many commitments already to add the commitment of a job. Besides, if she were going to spend more time in the public eye, she'd need clothes, suits, coats. A job could be a very expensive proposition. The income she made from her classes would have to be enough. Sure, she had those occasional weeks when some organization like Bomatumbi Mabatata's matrix regression therapy troup wanted to rent the entire island. That did add a little to the bottom line, but those requests, frankly, were few and far between and she could never anticipate when one of those groups would come up. She'd have to make the little steady income she had last. She could accept all of the dinner invitations she got and try to bring home doggie bags. That made no sense. If she accepted dinner invitations, she'd only have to reciprocate. Surely, there must be something. She banged the drum, grunted and pondered, grunted and pondered. "RRRR".

She had that job offer from Edith Kelly, but knew she could never make it work. How could she, Marla Saltonstall Stone, possibly ever in a million years make bacon wrapped scallops and sweet and sour kielbasa for a caterer who insisted on Scotch taping to the grimy windows of her shop enormous Kelly green shamrocks and leaving them on year round. Month after month, as the tape curled and discolored, those lurid green monstrosities absorbed every smell and grease spatter coming out of that very questionable kitchen and advertised to everyone in Hammerston how infrequently the windows were washed. Not possible.

SWEET AND SOUR KIELBASA

1 ring Polish Kielbasa	1 (10 oz. jar) red currant jelly
1 tsp. Honey	1 large can pineapple chunks
1 tsp. Prepared mustard	

Cook Kielbasa in boiling water for 10 to 15 minutes or brown it in a skillet. Combine honey, mustard, jelly and pineapple in a large saucepan. Add Kielbasa and simmer over low heat for 15 minutes, stirring occasionally. Slice diagonally into one-inch pieces and serve with frilled toothpicks.

She didn't think she could ever sink so low as to even consider Patrick. Patrick the blind man. He had some money, but not enough to make a dent in her expenses. His little shop on Newbury Street did all right. All the important decorators and designers bought their shutters, shades and blinds from him. Albeit at inflated prices - he was, after all on Newbury Street. He was presentable enough and accompanied her when she needed to be seen with an escort. But, she couldn't imagine herself actually *with* him. The same joke told over and over and over could, after a while become grounds for murder or at the very least serious bodily injury. "Hi. It's Patrick the blind man." How many times could that be funny? "Tell the pilot to have a safe flight." Once is more than enough for that line. Marla, after all, had cut her teeth on Ledge's wit and snappy repartee. His quick retort was his stock in trade. He had his clients, the ladies at FART, wrapped around his little finger with his clever one-liners and slightly off-color double entendres. And, his health. Patrick was a hypochondriac. He had a pinched nerve in his neck; a bulging disc in his back; a slight tear in his left meniscus; sleep apnea; and, that horrible post nasal drip. All that snorting. When he couldn't find a support group for PND, he'd thought of founding one himself, but had recently moved on to explore the possibility that he might be suffering from restless leg syndrome.

All the money in the world could never make Patrick the blind man even vaguely suitable as a life partner. Well, maybe *all* the money in the world. In the meantime, he looked good in a tuxedo, photographed well, the sex was better than nothing and Marla didn't have to spend that much time talking to him.

"Con permisso, Missus." Acumulada stood in the doorway. Marla had once purchased Spanish language audio tapes and had retained about five or six phrases. Acumulada, whose English was flawless with only the hint of an accent, always tried to use a Spanish phrase that Marla knew. She knew her employer enjoyed feeling bilingual.

"I know you don't like to be interrupted when you're banging, but I need to ask you something."

Marla came to from her reverie and gazed into the beady little eyes of her loyal housekeeper. She always tried to lock her gaze onto Acumulada's eyes. If she allowed her eyes to wander at all, they would invariably latch onto those gold teeth, the gold weather forecasting teeth, the teeth that seemed to catch and reflect light from every imaginable angle. It was better to stare directly into her eyes than at those mesmerizing teeth.

"What is it, Acumulada?"

"The water, Missus. It's boiling too much. Do you want me to turn it off?"

"Oh, thanks, Cara mia. Please."

"Sometimes you don't pay attention, Missus. It's a good thing I'm here for you. Sometimes you don't pay attention."

"You're right. Anything else?"

"Well, si. It's my sister, Maria Elena del Rio Candelario. She's here. She came to the States to have her eyes done. The cataracts are finally ripe. Her daughter has no room for her. With all those kids, how could anyone expect her to have room? I hate to ask you, Missus, but I told her I would. I told her I'd ask you if she could stay here with me. In my rooms. She'll be no trouble. It would only be for a week or so. No longer. She doesn't eat any more than one meal a day. Even less than I eat, even less than you eat, Missus. Do you think it would be all right? All she'd need is a bed and breakfast for about a week. She's on the phone. Can I tell her it's all right? Por favor?"

A bed and breakfast.

CHAPTER 5

▼

He examined a little dry patch around his left eye and applied another dab of Kiehl's panthenol protein moisturizing face cream. Moisturizing was the most important part of his morning routine. At least for the face. He carefully assessed the face. He didn't look that bad for an old guy. Old. He was only 59. Fifty-nine is nothing. But, with all he'd accomplished, he felt as though he'd lived two or three lifetimes. Fifty-nine was definitely not old. Not in this day and age. He was sure he looked amazing. His skin was carefully tanned and bronzed; his salt and pepper hair was close to perfect. No one would ever dream they were plugs. And, just as soon as his scalp healed, he'd be able to use permanent hair color rather than this shampoo-in/shampoo-out shit the dermatologist insisted on. Once Jon Xavier was free to get those magic hands of his on this new hair and balance the color, it would be perfect.

In addition to his face, he took excellent care of the rest of the package - his body. It was a temple. He had a full diagnostic CAT scan every year. Did it matter that insurance would not cover the few grand it cost? That was the only way to ensure that there were no tumors lurking symptom-less, silently ready to erupt when least expected. He intended to keep it that way. He ate only organic vegetables, fish and an occasional free range chicken breast and limited himself to one Grey Goose martini (with extra olives) every night and, most importantly, the daily workouts. Without them, this body would turn to flab before his very eyes. The workouts were key. Forget the fact that his knees throbbed with every lunge and his shoulders burned with every military press. He had to do it; he had to work through the pain; he had to ignore all those old football injuries. The final result was worth it. The pleasure of admiring the drape of his custom made monogrammed shirts rendered every throb of his ragged knees, every throe of his battered shoulders worthwhile. He preferred working out in the nude so he could admire every ripple from every angle, but he had too many nosy staff people in and out of his house. He'd had a couple of near misses with a young intern and decided to compromise. His workout garb of choice was instead the tiniest of Speedos. He'd once overheard his assistant refer to his chosen workout garb as butt floss. That assistant was no longer with the company.

He adjusted the weight on the universal machine and walked across the room to raise the volume on the CD player. Couldn't get too much of The Stones, not when you were working the pecs. His pecs were in good shape. If only he could do something about those nipples.

JET – Jack Egleston Trumpet. The monogram on the cuffs of those shirts. Jack Egleston Trumpet – CEO, well, soon to be CEO if the damn company could ever go public, if the market would only turn around and they could make their IPO, if he could get Barbie to sign off, then he could unload this turkey and cash in. He wouldn't sell all of his Conglomotron stock right away, only enough to buy that house on the south shore of St. Barts and the little boat. He'd have to keep the apartment in Boston and the house on the Vineyard, but he could get off this treadmill, this rat race and take his rightful place in society as patron of the arts, as a philanthropist. St. Barts was just the place to do it. He could walk in, set up shop, write a couple of big fat checks, one to the Battered Women's Shelter; one to their version of a college; and one to a museum or two and he'd instantly become a big man, a big fish in a small pond. He'd get the respect he was entitled to. They'd name a building after him, maybe two. Finally. It was never going to happen in this damn town. Sure, they'd take his money, the pols, the charities, the schools, but, do anything for him, forget about it. No matter how much he gave, no matter how much he tried to fit in, no matter how many clubs he paid dues to, he would never be a Kennedy or a Buffet. He was still the kid from the wrong side of the tracks in Covington Kentucky. Goddamn Covington, the armpit of the world. That place made Cincinnati look good.

Geez, those pecs are looking good. Nobody in Covington, Kentucky has pecs as good as these. But, the nipples. Couldn't somebody dream up some surgery or something for nipples? He had nipples the size of a CD ROM. The one fatal flaw in an otherwise perfect physique. Needless to say, his shirtless appearances were never public.

"I can't get no" … Nothing. The Stones were suddenly silenced.

"I need you to do this Jackie. I need it now."

His reverie was broken. Barbie's nasal twang jolted him back to reality. Now. Now. Not later. Everything had to be right now for her. Why couldn't it wait a few minutes, a few days, a few weeks. The woman had no patience. It's too bad Lenny hadn't taught her more patience when she was growing up. He'd been so focused on starting this company, on getting it off the ground, on building Conglomotron up to where it was today, he had no time for anything to do with his daughter. Sure, he gave her Conglomotron, but that was it. When she was a kid, it took less time to just give her anything she wanted. She'd whine that reedy honk and Lenny would write a check. A real time saver. It wasn't until Jack joined the company and married the boss's daughter that Barbie had ever heard the word "No". She'd heard it, but it had no meaning for her. Besides, it was usually coming out of her mouth.

"Jack, this is my career I'm talking about. I need you to do this now."

Her career. Right. Her career was nothing. It never had been. Her career was to wear the jewelry and clothes, shut her mouth and look good on his arm when he walked into a room. That was her career. Nothing more.

"Pile that blonde hair on your head, bleach your teeth, have your eyes done every few years and keep the weight off – that's your career."

Could he ever say that? Could he say that to the poor old girl?

Barbie genuinely thought this was going to work out for her. The movie roles he'd gotten for her had been dead ends. After one appearance, even his influence and strong-arm tactics were not enough to pressure any studio execs to sign her up for an encore. The big screen was not her future. TV. That's where she saw herself. A weekly show. No singing, no dancing, no heavy drama. She would do a lifestyle show. She'd teach the great unwashed masses how to live, how to live the way she did. She'd teach them what was wrong with their lives and how they could fix it by artfully arranging peonies, decoupaging a wooden chest, roasting the perfect free range chicken and making their own tab top curtains. There was only one wrinkle. Anytime Barbie wanted artfully arranged peonies, a decoupaged wooden chest, a perfectly roasted chicken or, heaven forbid, tab top curtains, she called a professional. She had the idea for the show, the concept for the show. What she didn't have was the talent. But, that had never stopped her.

Jack would have to do this for her. He had promised. Conglomotron had just bought that cable station. He controlled Conglomotron. She controlled Jack.

"I'm not even dressed. Can't it wait?"

"I don't think so. I'm sick of waiting. I've let it wait before. It has to be now."

She handed him a Burberry raincoat and pushed him out the door. "Your car is running."

CHAPTER 6

▼

A bed and breakfast! What an inspired idea. She certainly had the room and who better than she to make even the fussiest feel welcome and pampered. It would be an exclusive little hideaway, available only to a select few. Euro-trash visiting their Boston University sons and daughters; Middle Eastern sheiks scoping Boston real estate; South American businessmen shopping for medical care; wealthy Japanese evaluating the plants of the companies they'd just acquired. This would be her clientele. There would be no white-Nike-shod tourists arriving from Nebraska via Greyhound who'd come to walk the Freedom Trail. No camera wearing, fast-food eating tourists who'd driven down from the Canadian provinces. No *The Price is Right* grand prize winners touring the East Coast. No. She, with the help of Acumulada could pull this off. Maybe she could convince Maria Elena to stay after her cataract surgery to help her sister. There would be no advertising – word of mouth and maybe a quiet, discreetly placed notice in Town & Country would be more than enough. Some of Mother's old friends could come in very handy. She could charge exorbitantly and no one would care, not the kind of people she'd be catering to. Her guests would have all the conveniences of a five star hotel with the privacy of their own spacious home on their own private island. They could bring their dogs or cats or pet reptiles if they wanted to. It didn't matter. Acumulada could manage. She could manage anything. The guests would be thrilled. There'd be no gawking public they'd have to deal with. No doormen pretending not to be impressed by the fame of the people walking through their doors.

One or two guests a month would be enough to put her in the black. Was "guest" the appropriate word? After all, hotels called their paying customers "guests". There had to be a better word – something that would make people feel special, extraordinary. She'd come up with something, she was sure.

The transition to a bed-and-breakfast would be simple. She was already essentially set up for it, what with the separate bedroom suites she'd designed for Charles and Billy and the hordes of their college friends who'd descended on them every vacation. The separate entrance and that wing's access to the pool, stables, dressage ring, gym and tennis courts would make it ideal. The guests could stay in those suites and Acumulada and Maria Elena could serve the meals in the dining room.

If they had their own cars, they could use that enormous garage out back. Ledge was never what one would call a mechanical genius. He did, though, spend a fair amount of time designing a giant rotating turntable, a vehicular Lazy Susan that could accommodate 16 or 18 cars. It actually worked – most of the time. One car was driven into the garage when the turntable was in a position where an available space was lined up with the door. The turntable then was moved to its next position with the next space lined up with the door, and so on. Thus was he able to house his extensive collection of Silver Clouds, Citroens and Porsches. It was a clever idea. It took a fair amount of time and jockeying to get cars in and out of their berths, but to Ledge, it was certainly worth it. These babies were never to be exposed to the elements. Even though the garage was now emptied of Ledge's prize possessions, Marla usually left her Range Rover on the driveway. She never really trusted that Rube Goldberg contraption. It creaked and groaned and scraped with every rotation. Marla was sure she could notice the lights dim every time that lever was hit.

If a guest didn't have a car Guido could double as driver and borrow a Bentley from a neighbor. In some towns, neighbors borrowed a cup of sugar. Here in Hammerston, borrowing a Bentley was hardly unheard of.

Having paying guests would hardly interfere with her class schedule. She could prepare some components of the meals with her Tuesday food styling and presentation class. This was a stroke of genius. Of course, she should have the pool redone, but that could wait until the weather warmed up. The bedrooms Charles and Billy had grown up in would absolutely need to be redecorated. College kids, even on a part time basis, could never be accused of being careful of the Berber. And, the furniture would have to be replaced. What was appropriate for college students would never do for her guests. The marble baths were still in almost perfect condition. Except for that one leak. No, no she would have that ceiling redone. The fresco on the south wall wouldn't survive if the ceiling had to go, but she could probably get Albert the muralist to re-do it and stall him on the payment. He was, as most artists are, a notoriously bad businessman. The kids (when they came home) could stay in her wing. A couple of her sitting rooms could be set up as bedrooms for the boys. They were hardly ever at home anymore anyway. They might actually enjoy doubling up with Fernando and Carlos in Acumulada's wing.

But, where would the initial seed money come from? What if a good nor'easter came in from just the right angle and blew more of the roof off? What if Guido cracked some more of the cobblestones the next time he had to plow? What if the boiler decided to go at the very moment some Eurotrash clientele was stepping out of the shower? What if Patrick the blind man refused to sell to her at cost? What if, what if, what if?

CHAPTER 7

▼

"Just write it. Sit down and write it."

"What should I say? I don't know what to say".

Pam gnawed on her pencil stub. It was a habit she had picked up in second grade around the time Mrs. Kelly insisted she "get that pencil out" of her left hand and write with her right hand the way the Good Lord intended. Mrs. Kelly made perfect sense. If a person wanted to write, they should use their right hand. Write. Right. It was only natural. Besides, everyone knew the left hand was for the Devil's work. The study of Latin, as Mrs. Kelly presumably had done at her swanky East Coast college only served to further illuminate her position. Left: sinister; sinister: evil. It was as clear as the nose on one's face. Little Pam Yewlah had just better take that pencil out of her left hand and sit back and learn the Palmer Method with her right hand or that left hand would be secured behind her back. It was for the best.

"Come on, Pam, honey. Once you get started, it'll just flow. A few paragraphs, a short bio, that's all they want. I'll fix the spelling and grammar."

"Should I tell the truth?"

"Just write it". Fuller took a final look at his Palm Pilot before he slipped it into his attaché case. He checked the battery in his cell phone and headed for the door.

"I'll call you from the office."

Just write it? What should she say? What kind of club needed an essay as part of the application? What kind of club was named "The Club?" Clubs had names

– The Charles River Club, The Boston Social Club, The Beacon Hill Club. The Club. What kind of a place called itself that?

Oh, the people were nice enough. The ones she'd met, anyway. Florence Bainbridge, Ledge Stone's wife Marla, Suze and Larry. They seemed nice enough. But, everyone seemed to have known one another since birth. Even though Ledge Stone had been dead for years, he was still part of The Club, a presence. They all talked about him like he was away for the weekend and he'd be right back. They'd all gone to school together, to Andover or Choate. Then, they'd all gone to Harvard and Dartmouth and Yale and laughed about who won which football game which year. She could have gone to Harvard or Dartmouth or Yale, too, if she'd had the chance. Not too many kids from South Central Albuquerque High (Home of the Bulldogs) ended up at Harvard or Dartmouth or Yale, but she could have if only she'd had the chance.

She was smart enough. She was just as smart as they were. If only her Daddy's emu farm had been bought by Conglomotron the way it was supposed to be. The guy had promised him. Poor Daddy had sunk everything he had into emus. He was convinced they were going to be the wave of the future, the solution to so many of society's problems. One creature, one beautiful emu, could provide meat, eggs, leather, high quality guano. The guy from Conglomotron had promised. Daddy's farm was the next in line to be acquired. If it had happened, it would have meant a big cash payment, stock options, a secure future, a ticket out. Daddy would have been free to pursue his dream of devoting full-time to choreography – his God given gift. She could have left South Central – Home of the Bulldogs – and gotten a good college preparatory education and applied to Harvard, Dartmouth or Yale.

But, no, Mr. Jack Trumpet, President Jack Trumpet had seen to that. He'd seen to it that none of that was going to happen. Mr. Jack Trumpet decided the economic climate had reversed and in order to more appropriately expend the company's resources to deliver better value to consumers and shareholders, the emu acquisition program was being discontinued. "Thanks, Mr. Yewlah, but your emu ranch will no longer be on our acquisition list." That's what the letter said. "No longer be on our acquisition list."

Poor Daddy. Poor Mama. Poor Pam.

They never found Daddy's body – only the note. They were never even sure if he'd really killed himself. They'd consulted a suicidologist, but she was no help. Maybe if she had had more practical experience, the suicidologist would have been more helpful. Maybe if she'd been closer to finishing her training, she could have given them some ideas. But, since she was still a suicidologist in training, she just shrugged her shoulders patted Mama's hand and handed them her bill. That was the best they could do back home in Albuquerque. Pam was sure Daddy was still alive somewhere and only tried to set things up so that Mama and Pam could collect the $5,000 in final expenses insurance he'd left them. Pam felt he was living a new life far away from Albuquerque and emus and would one day return to her. Pam stayed at South Central where she cheered for the Bulldogs for four years. She could have applied to Harvard or Dartmouth or Yale and cheered for the Crimson, Big Green or Bullldogs, but, instead, stayed with Mama in the doublewide and spent her free time canning with Mama up around Santa Fe. It was pretty amazing how many returnables those gallery owners and rich folks just dropped in their trash barrels without even giving it a second thought. Five cents each.

The Club wants to know all about her. They already know everything about Fuller. They've all known him since practically before he was born. Now, they want to know about her. They want to know how Fuller, who'd been surrounded all his life by orthodontically corrected blondes from Harvard and Dartmouth and Yale had ended up engaged to a back-up, understudy Dallas Cowboys Cheerleader, second runner up.

What should she write?

CHAPTER 8

▼

Either the tires were loose or the axle needed oil or perhaps the serpentine belt was starting to go. It was always something with these old clunkers, but at least it still ran. Her vehicles got her where she needed to go, which is more than she could say for those NASA people – cheats and liars. That's what they all were, cheats and liars.

The scream of the low-on-fluid power steering crescendoed, then faded as she skillfully angled the rusting van's nose down the center line between two parking spaces. People got too close in these lots. She didn't need any careless young kids whipping their doors open without a thought to whom they'd be hitting. She spent enough time and money at this place to use two spaces. People just got too darn close.

"Miss Noone! Good morning!" Jimmy's voice boomed from the back room. "What are you doing here? You should have called."

"I didn't know myself if I'd be coming, Jimmy. What with this weather. I had to wait and see for myself what the driving was like. Certainly couldn't rely on those forecasters. They work people into a frenzy. Give a snowstorm some kind of name, especially this time of year, the March Monster or the Spring Surprise, Blizzard 06 – you'd think you were at Diary Queen – and it's own theme music. Then they tempt and tease and tempt and tease. We'll be right back with the forecast. Stay tuned for the forecast. Right after these messages. Messages. That's what's important. The messages."

Lulu Noone's internal furnace was starting to thaw her frigid little body. She unwrapped the hand knitted scarf she'd coiled around her flabbily folded neck.

The rosacia across her nose and cheeks seemed to come alive and throb, keeping pace with her flaring passion.

"Messages! Those people! Those companies! They're all cheats and liars! This snow is nothing. I barely had to shovel out. These people don't know what a snowstorm is. Probably don't even remember '78."

"It is supposed to get worse, though, they say. Maybe some flooding."

"Yeah, sure. Flooding. What will they dream up that rhymes with flood? Crud? Dud? Don't believe them, Jimmy, they're all cheats and liars."

Jimmy attempted to quiet her. His attempts were subtle, practiced. He'd seen this before. He guided the pudgy little creature to a plastic chair in the corner, her chair.

"I've got a nice cuppa tea, Miss Noone. You sit down right here and I'll bring it to ya."

"Oh, Jimmy, you're a good man." She'd begun to relax. Her face was cooling down to fuscia. "I wish I'd met a good man like you when I was a girl. Your wife sure is a lucky one."

"You know I'm not married, Miss Noone." The game was afoot.

"Oops, that's right. I forgot. I'm so silly." Her sparse eyelashes fluttered across watery pale blue eyes. In her mind she was Scarlett O'Hara at Twelve Oaks. Scarlett, though, never had to try to remember to keep her roots dyed that vibrant shade of red and never had to deal with varicose veins, bursitis and a distinct and growing more and more noticeable hearing loss.

Jimmy poured tea into a styrofoam cup and, after adding a little milk and sugar, handed it to his guest. "Now, Miss Noone, what can I do for you this morning? You're my only customer. Nobody's coming out in this weather. You've got me all to yourself".

Jimmy, who was young enough to be Lulu Noone's son if not grandson, was always made uncomfortable by her little flirtations. But, the customer was always right. He'd learned that from his father, the original Neon Jimmy. Neon Jimmy, Sr. had serviced most of the bars and restaurants in Boston and had quite a reputation as a ladies' man. Jimmy, Jr. had often wondered if anything had ever gone on between his dad and this very available old lady.

"I need some neon, Jimmy." She giggled, always amusing herself by what she thought an original joke.

"That's what I'm here for, Miss N. That's me, Neon Jimmy." He felt self-satisfied in his ability to calm her down based on the reading on the thermometer that was her face. But, the fact that the flaring face had subsided and the effect had shifted from livid to coquette had little to do with Jimmy's charms. Lulu

Noone was simply a victim of wild mood swings. Hormonal? Chemical? Congenital? Who knew? Lulu Noone was truly a multi-faceted woman. She'd long forgotten about the weather and the duplicity of forecasters and was now totally focused on the acquisition of the appropriate neon to complete her latest batch of paintings.

"I've got some new pieces in the van, Jimmy. They need the tubes installed."

"Sure thing, Miss Noone. I think we probably have some left in the back. I'll check."

"Some left in the back? What are you talking about. Left in the back? This is my neon tubing. This is where it is. This is where I get it. It must be plentiful; it must be in the front of the store. Available to me. I need to see it, to touch it."

Her rosacia was beginning to light up her face.

Jimmy scrambled. "I'm sure we have some, Miss Noone. Don't worry, we have plenty left."

"What do you mean 'left', Jimmy. You have plenty *left?* Is there something I should know?"

Jimmy spoke directly to his belt buckle. Better to just say it and get it over with. Take his punishment. He had dreaded her finding out – he knew she wouldn't be happy but, he had no idea that the news would upset her to this extent.

"They've discontinued that tubing, Miss Noone".

"Discontinued!!"

He took a breath. "But, I've got something almost exactly the same. Might even be better."

"Discontinued? Who discontinued my tubing? The distributor?"

"They're not making it anymore, Miss N. Not much call for that stuff now. Believe me, though, this new stuff, you're gonna like. Let me show it to you." He wanted to touch her, to pat her shoulders, to be sure she wasn't levitating off the ground, but, he dared not. He'd once gotten close enough to be within reach, but that smell, that wet saltine crackers smell that permeated her clothes, hair – that smell.

"I don't want new stuff, Jimmy." Her voice assumed an eerie calm, but her flaming cheeks betrayed her. "I don't want the new (she spat the word) *stuff*. I want the *stuff* I've always gotten here and I want it any time I want it. Do I make myself clear?"

"Look, Miss Noone, I'll do what I can. I'll look in the back. I'll give you what I have. I won't even charge you. I don't know if they're the colors you want. But, whatever I have I'll give you." He gripped the counter. "Hey, I've got a new shipment of baseball hats. Neon Jimmy baseball hats. Do you want one? A few? Whaddya say. I got them in lottsa colors?"

"That's not good enough, though, is it Jimmy? That just won't do. A baseball hat just won't do the job."

Her face settled into a pattern of Barbie pink and her pale eyes narrowed. She picked at the tiny speck of iridescent tangerine polish that still clung to her right thumb nail. She was thinking.

"Who is responsible for this outrage?"

"The manufacturer?" He was a schoolboy who'd forgotten his homework, trying out a guessed answer.

"And, Jimmy, who is this manufacturer of which you speak?"

Jimmy thumbed through the dog eared pages of a loose leaf binder. He'd been given a golden opportunity to look up the right answer. He'd find it. And fast. "Yeah, thought so. Conglomotron makes ... I guess I should say made those neon tubes."

The rosacia was once again in full flower. "Conglomotron! The snakes. They're doing this to me because I know. They've heard of me. They know that I know and now I'm being punished. And, now my art must suffer because of what I know."

"Because of what you know?" Jimmy's voice betrayed his loss of interest in this whole line of conversation with this dotty old lady. He'd found out the answer to her question. He was off the hook. Now, let's drop it. He was hoping desperately that the phone would ring or a customer would come in or perhaps the building would burst into flames. Anything for an excuse to get away from her and the wet saltine smell. No one was coming into the shop on a miserable wet Saturday. His commercial customers came in during the week. He stayed open on Saturday strictly as a convenience for the odd retail customer like Lulu Noone. No one else would be in today. His only hope was spontaneous combustion.

"It's the moon landing, Jimmy. I know and they know I know."

His face was a blank.

"NASA never landed on the moon, Jimmy. It was all staged out there in Area 51 out there in the desert. It was all a hoax perpetrated on American tax payers by Conglomotron and the rest of them. They built O rings for the rockets, they designed parts for the lunar lander and space suits. This moon landing meant billions for Conglomotron. But, we couldn't land on the moon, Jimmy. We never could have gotten through the radiation shield. The Russians knew it and gave it up. But, this moon program was a cash cow for Conglomotron. They'd invested tons of money in it and had to keep building and billing. 'Course, NASA and all those crooked pols were in their pockets. So, when they realized that all their rockets could never get there, they cooked up this scam. Staged what looked like a lunar landing in Arizona or Texas or Nevada, wherever Area 51 is, and we all fell for it. Well, not exactly all. I knew. I knew it was a hoax. I've been an artist all my life. I've been a keen observer all my life. I see things. I look at things. I remember things. That flag they planted – fluttering in the breeze? Any breeze on the moon, Jimmy? Can there be a breeze on the moon, Jimmy?"

"Ah, um" Again, he'd forgotten to do his homework.

"That's right, Jimmy. There is no breeze on the moon. With all of their weather satellites you'd think they'd know that, wouldn't you? Funny that they'd make that kind of mistake. Funny that their fatal mistake had to do with weather. With all their weather forecasters, meteorologists, indeed. All those weather theme songs. All those storm cams, weather tracks. Hmph. But, all their weather satellites are phony too. Phony satellites beaming phony pictures", she made quotation marks with the first two fingers of each hand, "back to earth. Those weather satellites are made by Conglomotron too, you know. They're beaming phony pictures to TV stations owned by Conglomotron so Conglomotron can charge more for airing Conglomotron's competitors' commercials. If anything, those satellites just watch us, watch what we're doing and keep it on our permanent records. Oh, it's a sweet deal, Jimmy. But, I'm on to them. They haven't got me fooled."

"Miss Noone?"

"So, they found out and this is how they punish me. By discontinuing my neon. But, they won't get away with this abomination. As God is my witness, that odious man will not get away with any of this."

"Miss Noone, do you want me to get some stuff from the back?"

Jimmy spoke too late. The fringe of the recoiled scarf whipped around the corner and Lulu Noone was out the door into the rain before Jimmy could stop her.

CHAPTER 9

---▼---

"Acumulada, you've simply got to turn that off and help. I cannot do everything at once. We've got the Club here tonight and the snow is starting to change to rain; I think I hear the sump pumps in the garage. I don't think I can stand another flood in the basement. Can't you miss that program for one day?"

We will return with part two of Guiding Light in a moment. Could that sonorous voice be taught? Its owner had to have been born with it. It boomed across the kitchen.

"This is my lunch hour, Missus, but I'll give you the commercials."

"The commercials!?"

"You can get a lot done in the commercials."

"Can't you miss it for one day?"

"The last time I missed one day, Susan and Max burned down Buzz's diner and no one had anywhere to go for dinner and Dinah shot Hart because she found out he was going back with Cassie. When I don't watch, things happen. I'm worried about Reva and Edmond. I'll give you the commercials."

"Oh, forget it. Take your full lunch. But, after it's over, we're getting this place ready for tonight. Addie's bringing a couple of new members. So, we'll be twelve for dinner with four more for dessert. Maybe 13 if Lulu Noone decides to show up. You know how she is. The Bodines are having dinner with the Youngs so they'll only be able to join us later to meet everyone. I think we'll do the Queen Mother's cake and Irish coffees. So, set up the library for 16, no 17."

"Missus, I can add thirteen and four. Don't worry. I'll do it in the commercials."

"I think we'll do a halibut." She hesitated, pondering. "Maybe with pistachios. That should work but we'll need to call to find out when the boat's coming in. If that fish sat on a boat too long ... and maybe a gazpacho. But, if that fish sat on a boat too long ... but, we won't know that until later this afternoon."

Acumulada Candelario muted her TV. Philip and Harley and Prince Edmund of San Cristobel were in pantomime. She slipped on her backless Versace high heel mules and teetered across the kitchen to her employer.

"Missus, are you all right? You never seem so tense. Are you all right? Que pasa?"

Marla gazed into the Maybelline mascared eyes of her housekeeper. Her all-Versace-clad housekeeper. Skintight red jacquard ankle length Capri pants, rhinestone studded V-neck spandex T-shirt and those electric blue three-inch mules. She sighed in resignation and smoothed the collar of her Old Navy turtleneck.

"Acumulada, where's your uniform?"

"This is my lunch hour Missus. I wear what I want."

"For an hour?"

"I wear what I want. Beth and Reva wear beautiful clothes all day, why shouldn't I when I watch?"

"In those clothes, all I can think of is Florence Bainbridge."

"That's where they came from, Missus."

"She gave them to you?" Marla was incredulous. That slut. The lover of her now dead ex-husband, the woman who probably had him murdered and stuffed into the trunk of her car, the woman who more than anyone else Marla could think of right now, was responsible for her current financial woes, she was giving her housekeeper her last season hand me downs.

"Not Mrs. Florence, Carmen Gloria. All the things you give me, Eileen Fisher, Ellen Tracy, Donna Karen, Anne Klein, they look better on Carmen Gloria and she can't get into any of Mrs. Florence's things. I can. We swap."

She struck her version of a glamorous pose. Only the tips of her gold front teeth were visible through her seductive pouty half smile. "I look good. I'm still skinny."

"For an hour? You put those things on for one hour?"

"I wear what I want and I watch what I want. This is my lunch hour." But, her determination was waning. She couldn't ignore Marla's anguish. "I shouldn't do this, but today for you special, I'll tape the rest to watch it later."

"Couldn't you always do that?"

"It's not the same. But, today, I'll make an exception. Why are you so crabby, Missus?"

Marla collapsed onto a Queen Anne kitchen chair and let her head fall dejectedly into her hands. Before she spoke, she rubbed her hands together and, noticing she'd forgotten to moisturize in the last hour, she bounced back up and took care of that little of detail. There could never be enough moisture in Marla's life. She regained her train of thought, remembering her desperation.

"It's so humiliating. She reached over to sniff the star-gazer lilies that had finally been delivered.

"The pollen will have to be removed from every one of these before I make my arrangements, Acumulada. I can't have orange powder dropping all over the tablecloth."

"Is the pollen humiliating?"

"Well yes, orange pollen all over my guests' noses would never do, but, as usual, you're right. It's not really the pollen I'm worried about. It's money." She could barely bring herself to say the words.

"In exchange for hosting this dinner, the membership committee is giving me a pass on my dues this year. I'm actually a charity case. Can you believe it? They've even offered to reimburse me for the cost of the food. Not that I'd even in a million years take them up on it."

"It's been a while since I've seen too many dineros, Missus."

"You know I'll always find a way to take care of you, Acumulada. I always have." She paused. "You've been poor before, but this is a whole new experience for me. I'm not sure I know how I can handle it."

"Do you need your tea, Missus, or your drum?"

Marla ignored Acumulada's offer. She was lost in thought.

"Those damn Coolidges. Ever since Addie got the idea in her head that Walter's family is descended from Pocahontas, they've been even more condescending than usual. All of that Native American garb and talking about a casino on the tribal lands. Those people are positively mad. Addie says that she feels the pain of the oppressed now that she knows how her people suffered so, she recommended to the Board that I be given a pass on the dues this year. She, Addie Coolidge, that madwoman, is feeling my pain. I've never been so humiliated in my life. I'm mortified by a lunatic and I have to take it. I have no choice, do I?"

"You could resign."

Marla had been a member of The Club since, … when? Before she was born? Her parents had been members as had her grandparents. Ledge, too, had grown up at The Club. How could she function without The Club? Resignation was not an option. No. She had to take the handouts of idiots like Addie Coolidge – accept their charity.

"You do a lot for that club, Missus".

"Yes I do, goddamn it."

"And for this neighborhood and town, too". Acumulada's loyalty to her employer was legendary. Her lack of a salary for the last several months was not a factor. The only thing that she cared about and truly cared about was Marla's security and happiness and position in the community.

"And for this neighborhood too."

"Did they ever offer you anything for your newsletter? For the paper and the stamps, forget about your time and my time?"

"Never". Marla's shame at becoming a charity case was beginning to evolve into sanctimonious outrage at the ingrates she counted among so many of her "friends".

"It's not like it's a lot of money, but they could have offered. It's the principle of the thing. They always thank me, of course, but they could have offered. This dinner alone is costing me a small fortune. And, this is money I don't have any-more."

"Tell me about it." Acumulada filled the kettle and put it on to boil. "Missus, I'll make your tea. Do you want your drum? Would that make you feel better?"

"You know, I think maybe a little more drumming would be a good idea." She headed for the stairs. "You finish watching your story, Acumulada, I'll be upstairs."

*   *   *   *

QUEEN MOTHER'S CAKE

6 ozs. Sweet German chocolate coarsely cut	*¾ cup butter*
¾ cup sugar	*6 eggs, separated*
6 ozs. almonds, finely ground	*pinch of salt*

Line bottom of buttered spring form pan with parchment paper. Butter paper and dust with fine bread crumbs. Melt chocolate over hot (not boiling) water in double boiler. Allow to cool slightly. Cream butter and sugar and beat at moderately high speed for thee minutes. Add egg yolks one at a time, beating after each addition. Beat in cooled chocolate. At low speed, gradually beat in ground almonds. In a separate bowl, beat egg whites until stiff, but not dry. Fold the whites into the chocolate mixture in thirds. Turn into prepared pan. Bake in lower third of oven for 20 minutes at 375. Reduce oven temperature to 350 and bake an additional 50 minutes. After 70 minutes (total) remove from oven and place pan on a damp towel. Let stand for 20 minutes. Remove sides of springform. Cover with a rack and invert. Carefully remove bottom of pan. Cover with another rack and invert again to cool right side up.

Icing

½ cup heavy cream   *2 tsps. Instant coffee*

8 ozs. Sweet chocolate (Tobler) coarsely broken

Scald cream in heavy saucepan over medium heat. Add instant coffee and whisk briskly until dissolved. Add chocolate and heat for one minute. Remove from heat and whisk until chocolate is melted and mixture is smooth. Place pan in cold water to stop cooking. Let stand for 15 minutes, stirring occasionally until icing comes to room temperature. Pour over top of cake, letting a bit run down the side.

CHAPTER 10

▼

"Hey, good morning neighbor! Inside! Hey, anybody home?"

Acumulada clicked across the terra cotta in her backless Versaces. Missus Marla was getting a little careless. She had left the front door wide open. Anybody could walk right in and, anybody did. For one of the few times in her life, Acumulada del Rio Maria Candelario was speechless in both of her languages. The Burberry trench coat hung casually unbuttoned over a fire engine red spandex Speedo. The man wore it with such grace and lack of embarrassment that one could only assume that he actually thought he looked good. Apparently, he had the kind of mirrors that did not reflect paunch and droop. The muffler which matched the raincoat lining hung from his neck and created a weird X across his chest which accentuated his rather grotesque appearance. The scarf also served as a border, for the two enormous nipples that sat like an order from IHOP on his chest. The more he worked out, the bigger those nipples seemed to become. He was sporting two brown saucers on his hairless chest. The only way he could deal with this odd imperfection was to convince himself, and thereby convince others that it was in fact, a blessing, a sign that he'd been marked for greatness among mortals. He'd convinced exactly half of his desired audience.

He grinned exposing perfect veneered teeth and removed his Christian Dior green aviator glasses. The glasses had been shielding tiny symmetrical laugh lines at the corners of his china blue laser corrected eyes. The eyes bore into Acumulada as he approached, both hands extended. He clasped her hand in his right and, with his left circled her wrist in that classic politician's handshake, the one that says "I'm really, really happy to meet you and I'm going to try really really hard to remember your name" The unbuttoned Burberry trench coat that covered little more than the back of his little red Speedo caused its wearer not one bit of embarrassment. It was as though he were covered from head to toe in a custom tailored three-piece chalk stripe suit.

"Great place you've got here". His eyes swept from the worn Perpedil prayer rug at his feet to the chipped paint on the frescoed ceiling. He lowered his voice conspiratorially. "I've got someone I want you to meet. A contractor. Forget contractor, this man is an artist, a true artist, an artist like from the Old World. He could do such a job for you here. Let me have him stop by."

Acumulada had met her share of egos both north and south of the border, but this one took the piñata.

"He can do wonders with these old places. Still keep the charm and all that, but get them up to code if you know what I'm saying."

She opened her mouth to speak, but it was Marla whose voice was heard.

"May I help you?" She had appeared silently from the staircase behind him.

Now it was Jack Trumpet's turn to be at a loss. His hesitation lasted only a nano second. Warmth and sincerity exuded from every pore. The recently corrected eyes swept from Versace to Eileen Fisher; from Eileen Fisher to Versace. Shit. How could he have made such a blunder? He laughed heartily.

"Did I put my foot in it or what!! Mrs. Stone, or may I call you Marla. Jack. Jack Trumpet. What a pleasure to meet you."

He repeated the practiced politician's arm grip handshake, this time upon his intended recipient, turning 180 degrees away from the Versace clad Acumulada.

"This is more like it". He inched just a little closer, lowering his voice, but not quite enough to render it inaudible to Acumulada. I should have recognized a woman like you, with your reputation and all. That dress and that dental work. You must pay your help very well. Meanwhile, I can't believe I made such a mistake. Say you'll forgive me."

Marla's years of marriage to Ledge had given her every opportunity to practice and perfect the art of jackass nonreaction. For her to stand there and stonily watch this vision in red spandex without convulsing into laughter was like breaking sticks. She did, though, need to steel every fiber of her being to keep her eyes focused anywhere but the pancake sized nipples and his miniature perpetually flickering hands.

PANCAKES

2 cups flour	*1 tsp. baking soda*
1 tsp. Salt	*2 cups buttermilk*
3 eggs, separated	*¼ butter, melted*

Sift flour with salt and soda. Stir in egg yolks and buttermilk. Add butter and beat well. In a separate bowl, beat egg whites and gently fold into batter. Drop by spoonfuls onto hot greased griddle. They are ready to turn when bubbles form and begin to break on surface.

She repeated "It's a pleasure to meet you, Mr. Trumpet, I had no idea you'd moved into Tweedy's old place so soon. Welcome. Welcome to Hammerston. I hope you'll be very happy here." She motioned him inside.

"Oh, Jack, please. We're neighbors. No need to be so formal."

"Jack, then." She smiled her most insincere smile. Dina Merrill had nothing on her. Marla turned to her housekeeper who was hovering between suspicion and incredulity. "Acumulada, is your lunch hour over?"

"Si, Missus. My program, she is finished", came the heavily accented reply. Acumulada had, for years, used her level of Spanish accent, mispronunciations and shattered syntax to try to telegraph messages to her employer. When she was relaying a phone message to Marla from her broker that a stock she'd held in her portfolio had tanked, she was Vicente Fox; when she was trying to break it to her gently that Charles had been put on academic probation at Essex, she was Carmen Miranda; when she was attempting to report Ledge's affair with Florence Bainbridge, she was positively Charo. Today, for some reason, that intermittent Spanish accent was breaking through. Marla didn't always make the connection. Right now, she had no time to wonder about Acumulada's little mind games. She had a party to prepare for and now this semi clad neighbor to entertain.

"Good, dear. Why don't you change your clothes and get started on the Queen Mother's Cake for tonight while Mr. Trumpet and I have", she paused, turning to her guest with a question in her voice, "coffee?"

"Don't go to any trouble for me, but if you have a Pelligrino, I'd love one. No ice, a chilled glass and a little slice of lemon, seeded."

"Missus, the cake she is made. She is over and finished. I did it last night. And, Missus, there is coffee and Pellegrino and chilled glasses with seeded lemons in the breakfast room. I did it in the commercials."

"How did you …? Oh, never mind. But, I do so hate it when you do that, Acumulada. How ever do you do it anyway? I'll never know. But, as long as it's done, maybe you could finish up the Hoovering before we finalize the place cards. There's a luv." Marla's use of affected Britishisms which she'd picked up during her Junior year in London reflected her anxiety level as clearly as did Acumulada's regression to Hispangibberish.

"Let's not stand here in this drafty parlor, then, Mr. er, Jack." Her Dina Merrill smile widened in response to her effort she needed to expend in order to resist the temptation to take his coat. "Shall we?" She was hoping he might explain his unusual ensemble. He said nothing; merely followed her into the dining room which was already set up for tonight's festivities. The Louis XV tulilpwood table was set, complete with place cards. As promised, Pellegrino, a lovely bucket of chilled glasses and a plate of seeded lemons sat beside the coffeepot on the sideboard.

"Unusual help you've got there". Jack Trumpet nodded in the general direction of the front hall, the scene of Acumulada's departure.

"She is a gem, n'est pas?"

He accepted the proffered Pelligrino and sipped. "N'est pas."

"So," she wracked her brain for conversational fodder while she fine tuned the color of her coffee. "When did you move in? I frankly lost the thread of some of our local goings on. I guess the closing on Tweedy's house just slipped right under my radar."

"I'm not the kind of guy who likes to wait for things. When I decide I want something, I make it happen. Some people might call it a fault. Impatience. I don't want to know about deferred gratification. I think of it more like action. A man of action. That's me. I heard Tweedy Fernald's house was on the market, made a full price offer and closed the following week. Like I said, I don't like to wait. Not for small deals like real estate. Act. That's my motto."

"Act. Um." Marla groped for small talk. She was beginning to regret having sent Acumulada away. This man, this Jack Trumpet was making her nervous. What did he want that was so urgent that he had to motor over here without even bothering to dress?

"Well, we're delighted to have you in our little neighborhood. Even though I'm out here on the island, I still feel like part of our village. I've read so much about you in the financial magazines. Conglomotron. It must be quite an exciting life, involved in all those elaborate multimillion dollar deals all around the world."

"You know something, honey, the excitement in life is what you make out of it. I feel just as excited hitting a perfect tee shot at St. Andrews as closing a major acquisition deal."

"St. Andrews?" Marla was beginning to be impressed. She'd always had a soft spot for golf. Such warm memories: her dad; spring afternoons; long velvety fairways. She really should try to play again this year. It had been such a long time. Would she ever again have enough free time to play golf?

"Life is always exciting for me. I see to it." As he spoke, one hand gripped the Pelligrino and the other began kneading his lambswool Burberry scarf. Marla was a little concerned that he might decide to take it off, leaving nothing but the raincoat between her and the red Spandex. He did no more than pull the bit of scarf up to his mouth and roll the wool between his fingers, like an anxious high speed baby getting that needed reassurance from his special well-loved blankie. He was suddenly coy. He almost whispered, "You haven't mentioned it, so I'm assuming you don't know."

"Don't know?" Marla was intrigued.

"I'm going to be here tonight. Right here in your house. Right here." He tried to clasp his little hands together in glee, but managed only a collision between his scarf and Pelligrino. "The Coolidges are bringing us, Barbie and me, proposing us for membership. Can you believe it, us, Jack and Barbie Trumpet, members of The Club?" He was suddenly modest, self-effacing, Mr. Middle America. "Well, we're just tickled pink."

"We're naturally, positively delighted you're able to make it tonight", Dina Merrill cooed.

Mr. Middle America disappeared and yet another of his personalities emerged. "Ha", he laughed. It came out as two breathy nasal syllables, rather than even an honest attempt at a genuine expression of humor. Diabolical, that is if Satan had been topless with nothing between the world and his enormous brown nipples but the fringes of a Burberry scarf. "Hope we get in."

"Well, why wouldn't you? We'd all be thrilled to have you and your lovely wife, Bobbie, is it?"

"Barbie. Her name is Barbie, like the doll. Barbie."

"Barbie, of course, how captivating. I'll be sure to remember that. I had a sorority sister named Barbara."

"Not Barbara. I said Barbie. Barbie. Here, let me show you. Maybe if you see it in print, you can remember."

Marla was really starting to worry. Where was Acumulada? How long would this person stay? She was positively horrified at her lack of manners by not even inviting him to sit, but she just couldn't encourage him. Trumpet placed his glass on the sideboard and reached into his raincoat and extracted an 8 x 10 glossy complete with vital statistics, credits and contact numbers. Barbie Lee Trumpet. A full headshot took up most of the photo, with smaller posed shots creating the border. Barbie Lee holding a puppy; Barbie Lee walking in the rain; Barbie Lee curled up on a window seat filling in the *New York Times* crossword puzzle. In each of the poses, Barbie was carefully and perfectly lit from the left, her bizarre mink eyelashes at half mast looking out at Marla over her left shoulder.

"Is she a", Marla groped for the right word, actress, model, spokesperson, what? "Professional?"

"You could say that. She's working at it and working very hard."

Marla studied the photo. Every feature was perfect, more than perfect. Impossibly perfect and yet, somehow, all the pieces didn't fit. All the pieces didn't add up to anything. They were just an assortment of perfect features arranged in the basic configuration of a face. But, lifeless. Like her namesake. It was as if five or six different plastic surgeons, all without the knowledge of one another, had been working independently yet simultaneously. Marla dared not look to see if her measurements which she was sure were included on the back of this photo composite corresponded to Mattel's idea of perfection.

"She has beautiful features." Marla didn't lie.

"She's a very talented little woman." Jack Trumpet did. "Her career just needs a little jump start, a little push in the right direction". He paused, running his tongue over his expensive dental work. "She needs some direction; some smart affiliations."

Marla had no idea what the man was talking about. She had intended merely to make small talk along the "how's-the-wife-and-kids" line and it had escalated into some sort of deep analysis of Barbie Lee Trumpet's goals, dreams and aspirations. She had no time for this. She had a party to prepare for, she had an appointment with Svetlana in an hour for her microdermabrasion facial and, goddamn it, she had a debt-ridden life to contend with. This guy could perhaps start paying to tell his troubles to a shrink or at the very least, knock himself out and throw some bloody clothes on before he went calling on neighbors and let her get on with it.

"She needs some smart affiliations. And, that's where you come in." He pulled a chair away from the table and looked to Marla. "May I?"

How could she refuse. He sat down, the Burberry trench coat spilling off to either side, exposing tanned knobby knees. He was sitting at the place designated for Addie. He picked up the heavy folded ecru card. "*Addie Coolidge*" inscribed in perfect calligraphy across the front. Acumulada, had, as usual, inscribed each place card in her perfect calligraphy and, had arranged them around the table.

"Love these little touches. It makes life so much easier when you know just where you're going to be tomorrow." He smiled. "A wonderful woman. Mrs. Coolidge. Native American, you know."

"Yes, I know." Yes, she knew.

"And, she's doing so much for her people. That museum of hers is going to be something. Barbie and I are lucky enough to be involved. We're feeling really blessed to be able to be a part of it."

Addie Coolidge and her recently discovered Native-American-by-marriage-heritage were topics of conversation that could easily wait until the cocktail hour tomorrow night when everyone was desperate for chit chat. What did this man want?

Trumpet was not to be distracted. "We might even be lucky enough to have a building named for us, for Barbie and me. That something?" He paused gazing longingly with his mind's eye into the space that would be Addie Coolidge's Native American Museum. "Maybe the wall at the entrance, *THE JACK AND BARBIE LEE TRUMPET WALL OF HOPE.*"

Ah, that was it. Marla had been wondering how much it was costing this clown to be proposed for membership by Addie and Walter. Now she had her answer. A building at their new museum. At least Addie didn't sell out cheap. In the old days, her dad had been the one who had buildings named for him. But, that was ancient history. Now, quality community leaders, people like Waldo Saltonstall had been replaced by this. She could barely control her revulsion. Besides gloating about how much money he had, what was this guy doing here?

"You mentioned Barbie's career?" Marla hoped she could direct the conversation away from the topic of his philanthropy.

"Her career, yes, but, more importantly, making smart affiliations. In business, we make mergers and acquisitions all the time. We merge two companies into one. We acquire smaller companies. We're acquired by larger companies. *De rerum natura.* The natural order of things.

If Marla didn't finish and get to Svetlana by 1:00, her whole schedule would be backed up and tonight's plans would be in a shambles. Her patience was running thin.

"What Barbie needs is a merger or perhaps we should call it an acquisition." He fingered the crease in Addie's place card as his eyes scanned the table. "Quite a crowd you've got coming. The beautiful people. People who know how to live."

Marla was not sure where he was going. And, although she said not one word, her face must have asked.

"My dear lady, my wife needs to acquire you."

"Acquire me!?" Marla was positively horrified. If Addie had wanted to really feel the pain of the oppressed, the downtrodden, the powerless, she should stand here and listen to this repulsive little man say he wanted to acquire her.

"Well, perhaps it would be more palatable for you to consider it a merger"

She was not following. This revolting creature with his red Speedo sitting at her dining room table with his nipples perilously close to actually touching her Wedgewood Silver Ermine chargers was talking about acquiring her.

"I'm quite sure I don't know what you mean."

"We", he stumbled a moment. "Conglomotron, that is. I feel it's such a part of me, I always call it 'we'." He paused and let escape his version of a giggle. "We've just put together a deal for a new cable channel, a sort of How-to channel. There's plenty of programming available already, but we need a linchpin, an anchor, something unique to help viewers identify with us." His tiny fingertips played pat-a-cake with one another, faster and faster as his excitement heightened. "What our new channel needs is a full length, daily lifestyle show on gardening, home decorating, food styling, birdsong recognition, herbal remedies, that sort of thing starring", he paused for effect and got it. "Starring Barbie Lee Trumpet".

Marla was not sure what kind of reaction was expected of her. Jack Trumpet was listing her classes, the classes she taught in this very house. Did Barbie have any expertise in any of these areas? Could she actually pull this off? Her upper lip stiffened as she replied, "That sounds very interesting."

"It'll be even more interesting, honey, when I tell you the rest of the plan." His little hands were spinning wildly. "I am about to offer you, Marla Stone, the in-cred-ible chance, the chance of a lifetime." He paused to heighten the anticipation. "The chance to sit in the co-host's seat."

He wasn't getting the response he'd expected. "Co-host the show!! Are you listening? Can you hear me? I'm offering you the job as co-host on Barbie's show. Whaddya say? This is going to be huge. I smell a winner. You'll be teaching your little classes, except you'll be teaching them to millions of viewers. No more little newsletter for you. This is big time honey."

Marla opened her mouth to register her shock, her horror. Co-hosting a daily television show with a brainless parasite. She'd been a *co* before. Co-president of the museum guild; co-chair of the ballet gala; co-author of the charity cookbook.

Co-host indeed! She knew what co meant. She'd end up doing all the work while Barbie was in hair and make up. Forget it.

Before she could respond, Jack silenced her with one of his tiny fingers which he pressed against her lips. "Don't answer now. I want you to think about it. I know it's a lot to digest, so to speak." He laughed mightily at his weak pun. "Think about it, honey. Don't answer right away. Call your lawyers. I'll fax the proposal over to them." He again reached into the bag of tricks that was his Burberry trench coat and pulled out several typed pages which, presumably, were said proposal. Marla would not have been at all surprised if he had a fax machine down deep in one of those pockets. "What time do they get in? Young & Young, right? Can I use your fax?"

Marla still had not responded. She was more than speechless. She was stunned. It was at times like this that Marla really regretted having given up cigarettes. Right about now, she could have lit up a Winston and taken those few seconds to pull herself together; to buy herself some time to respond. But, no, those days were gone. And now, this sleazy little peacock was suggesting that she, Marla Stone, should go on television; that she should teach her classes on television and allow anyone who owned a TV set to watch her; to listen to her; to use her recipes, her flower arranging tricks, her gardening tips, her decoupage techniques; her fung shei and herbal remedies. No, it was too much. The great unwashed, the great polyester wearing population having access to Marla Stone's lifestyle instruction. No, it was just too much to expect of anyone.

"You know, television is not really my sort of thing."

Jack Trumpet was a chameleon who could shift effortlessly from smarmy charmer to cut-throat enforcer. The enforcer spoke. "I've done my homework, honey. I know you need it. This is a big payday we're talking about, for both of us." Without even taking a breath, the smarmy charmer reappeared. "Think of what you can do to this place. What do you call it? Stone Hurl? You could fix it up the way it should be; you could fix that bridge; you could update the HVAC; you could have something to pass on to your boys; you could pay your taxes. You wouldn't want this place being sold for back taxes now, would you? Think of your boys, think of their future. You owe it to them."

Her boys. Marla did owe her boys. This was their legacy. She had chosen foolishly when she picked their father. The very least she could do was give them a financially secure future. But, didn't she also have an obligation to spare her boys the indignity of seeing their mother bare herself on national TV?

The enforcer pressed on. "The TV show would just be the beginning. I see a line of housewares, linens, cookbooks, gadgets, gardening tools, decoupage kits.

You two girls are going to become an industry. The two of you. But, I need your answer now. I need to go home and tell my little bride that you're on board here; that you've agreed. Thirteen weeks. That's all I ask."

Marla sank into the Chippendale armchair. Her voice was beginning to betray her weariness, her total exhaustion from the superhuman effort of staying afloat the last few years. She'd tried, she really had, but it was getting to be too much. How much longer could she be expected to shoulder it all? And the future. What future? She had no prospects. Things were destined to only go from bad to worse. "How long did you say?"

"Thirteen weeks"

Acumulada appeared in the doorway, perfectly turned out in her gray cotton day uniform and black New Balance cross trainers. On her silver tray sat two bone dry Grey Goose martinis, each with four olives.

"Was thinking you might want something, Missus."

The smarmy charmer grinned his grin. "I take it one of these is for me? Remarkable. How did you …?"

Acumulada's golden smile flickered then faded.

"Thirteen weeks?"

"Thirteen weeks."

Marla reached for her martini and stared into the eyes of her new employer.

CHAPTER 11

▼

"I'm going to lie down. Five minutes, that's all I need. I'm sure you'll understand if Acumulada shows you out."

"Power naps are the sign of true genius. Me, myself, I take a power nap just about every day. There's nothing more rejuvenating, more revitalizing."

This piece of information which Marla presumed was intended to make her feel better only served to reinforce the feeling that she had sunk to a new low. She now used the same coping strategies as this grotesque hairless artificially bronzed person.

Marla knew she should have been feeling very different feelings about what had just happened. Her life was about to change dramatically. Her financial problems were over, or at least the potential existed for them to be over sometime in the foreseeable future. It was a Tuesday in March, she'd had a martini before 5, she was going to be a no-show at Svetlana's and she was going back to bed. This was a first. She had sunk to a new low.

"I just need to process this."

"Mr. Trumper, is there something more?" Acumulada was doing her absolute best to be obsequious.

"That's Trumpet, like the horn, honey. People always say I'm pretty horny." He laughed nasally "Ha ha." Acumulada's lack of response compelled him to feel the need to explain. "That's a joke in English. You'll get English jokes soon. I'm sure. After you've been in the country a little longer."

"Si. Mr. Trump ette." Acumulada was making every attempt to shepherd him towards the door. Missus Marla had instructed her to show this man out and that was what she was going to do. Jack Trumpet made no moves in that direction, but instead, settled back in his chair. "Love these placecards. Does Mrs. Stone do this fancy writing herself?"

"Used to be Missus Marla she does it. But, she teach to me how. Now, I do it the writing. When it's over, she checks me to see who is where sitting."

He scanned the table and fingered several of the cards. "So great to be able to know where you're going to be. Makes life so much more civilized. Let's see. Walter here and Florence Bainbridge over there. Where am I? Where's Barbie? Where are we sitting?"

"I see your name on the list from the Indian squaw. I make you cards. You and Missus Bobbie. You in good seats."

Acumulada picked up the heavy ecru card, the card which would put Jack Trumpet to Marla's right. "Here you be, Mister. Right by Missus Marla." Acumulada was beginning to sound a lot like Mammy and needed to get away from this man before she forgot every word of English she ever knew. He was having a very negative effect on her accent.

"What about my bride? Where's she sitting?"

"Right here, Mister. She's right between Dr. Franklin and Mr. Bainbridge."

"That's not going to work for us Cumulus."

"Acumulada"

"Acumulada, of course, forgive me. That's not going to work for us because my wife is left handed, you see, and she'll have to be on the end. So, she'll change places with Addie. Yes, that will work." He stood back and admired his new arrangement.

"This is the way Missus Marla would want this table, Mister. I set it like she want it. I don't think she want it the other way."

"Nonsense, this will be fine. Now, you run along. I'll find the door."

CHAPTER 12

▼

"Where is that son of a bitch?? He can't do this to me. I was acquitted. You can't do this to an acquitted man. I was acquitted!! Fran had been old Mr. Young's secretary for close to 50 years and not once had she been forced to listen to this kind of language from a client or from anyone else. She tried hard to maintain the regal bearing that had been her stock in trade and she felt so accurately reflected the overall ambience at the law firm of Young, Young & Silverberg.

"Mr. Young is in a meeting, Mr. Quinn. I'm sure if he had any idea you'd be in, he would have cleared his calendar."

"I don't give a fuck about his calendar." He waved a handful of crumbled papers in her face. "I have a contract. That motherfucker can't do this to me. I have a fuckin contract. I am the spokes fuckin man for Conglomotron. I got a contract." He laid two ham sized arthritically gnarled black hands down on Fran's polished rosewood desk. He leaned forward to within inches of her face and gazed into her eyes. He whispered. "You get that motherfucker out here now or I'm goin' in there myself. Nobody terminates P. D. Quinn. I was acquited. goddammit." Fran's voice was barely a croak. "Mr. Young is only the lawyer. He was only doing what the client wanted."

CHAPTER 13

▼

People could say what they would about her, but Marla managed to pull it together and suck it up when she had to. After all, she'd had plenty of training. She'd entertained the best of them, from her parents' Brahmin friends and associates to Ledge's nouveau riche clients. Her own neighbors ran the gamut from impoverished nobility to a couple of very recently rich who were desperately trying to break into Hammerston society. The recently rich, of course, wouldn't ever succeed, everyone knew that. But one must never be rude and let on that one knew and, besides, it was such fun to watch them try so very hard to impress. The recently rich hired decorators; they consulted landscape architects; they bought books by the yard to fill their library shelves; they invested in art they knew nothing about; they leased horses and tried to teach their unattractive little children to ride; they bought shiny cars to impress valet parkers. None of it worked. They were still the recently rich and would remain so, at least for the next two or three generations.

Marla's real circle on the other hand didn't need decorators – they had the English furniture and Turkish rugs and Irish crystal and French porcelain and American silver the house had been furnished with when they'd inherited it. If something wore out or the slobbering Labs who dozed on the furniture or skidded across the rugs eventually did succeed in destroying something, it was taken care of - it was merely redone in the original damask or silk. Why try to improve on perfection? They were happy to ride in a ten-year old Chrysler just so long as someone else was doing the actual driving. They would rather spend their money endowing a chair or patronizing a promising young artist.

The impoverished nobility, on the other hand, were in a particularly difficult predicament. Unlike poor working people, or even the recently rich, they had an intuitive sense of what needed to be done and knew how it should be done properly. Unfortunately, they had that little cash flow problem. Turkish rugs and silk and damask and even Chryslers did not come cheap. It dawned on her suddenly that she, Marla Babcock Saltonstall Stone, was facing the prospect of joining that class, the impoverished nobility unless she took Jack Trumpet's offer. She'd said yes and that was that. Her only option was to momentarily throw her principles aside, prostitute herself and become a television personality. A public figure.

Things could be worse after all. She could still be married to Ledge. But, she wasn't and wasn't even collecting the ex-wife alimony anymore now that he'd bought the farm. She was just going to have to make it on her own. On her own with the help of the Trumpets. If that meant that television viewers in Ohio, would be able to learn her tricks for producing remarkably life-like paper flowers, her recipes for Chinese herbal remedies, and the proper techniques for repotting Bonsai jade plants, that's what it would be. She, though, vowed that she would be an oddity in the television business. She would demonstrate to the world that being a television "personality" did not mean casting one's dignity to the four winds. She would retain her poise and decorum at all times and perhaps show people in places like Ohio or even Montana just what gracious living was all about.

It really wasn't all that bad. She wasn't doing Jerry Springer, after all. She wasn't like them. Some people actually would do just about anything to get on television. People videotaped their child falling off a jungle gym to submit to a TV show on the off chance that theirs would be selected as the "funniest". If it were, of course, the blissfully happy little family – mom, dad and (now fully recovered from the fall) little child – could appear on the program and compete with others who'd videotaped grandpa being beaned by the stepped on garden rake or junior driving the car through the garage door. All for the privilege of being on television.

Television had a captivating effect. It was a flattering medium. People said it added ten pounds. For Marla, that was no problem. She was satisfied with what she looked like on those closed circuit security cameras at mall entrances. With hair and make up professionally done, yet, this could be a good thing.

She was really warming up to the idea. She'd do it for a while; she'd look marvelous and she'd be able to pay her debts. She didn't want to think about her prospects too far in the future lest she put the hex on things, but for the moment at least, things were looking up.

She knew she'd gotten a call from someone at Young, Young & Silverberg—she'd seen it on caller ID, but she hadn't the time to actually pick it up or even to listen to the message on her voice mail. Every minute of this day has been spoken for and she was absolutely unwilling to let any of her commitments suffer because of this unexpected complication. The call had been from Old Mr. Young, or young Mr. Young, maybe. It certainly wasn't Len Silverberg. As her father had done years before, she'd made it abundantly clear that he was never to be involved in her affairs in any way. But, someone at Y, Y & S had called; someone had gotten a fax or a call from Jack Trumpet; and, someone knew how much he was offering for her soul. Well, she'd show them that she could still own her soul no matter how much they were paying. She'd see old Mr. Young in a few hours when he presided over The Club membership meeting. That would be plenty of time. She was more than happy to wait.

A glance out the window. The snow that had started and stopped so many times yesterday and was now starting to change to rain. Acumulada had said that she'd prayed for it to change and, by God, it was changing. This was a real blessing. This was an omen. This meant things were starting to look up. More snow would have been such a nuisance. She had already asked Guido to stay on during the evening to be sure the guests' cars were brushed off and warmed up before they drove them the two or tree miles home. She could now let him leave once he put all the cars in the garage. He always loved using that fancy Rube Goldberg turntable contraption Ledge had designed so he could fit everyone's car indoors, all noses in towards the center of the pie. With the weather turning around, she could give him the evening off. He never would have complained. The man was a saint. But, things were going to be different around here from now on. Once she took this job, once she started actually earning money, she'd pay him and everybody else she owed. She'd start paying people the kind of money they deserved. Guido, Acumulada, Maria Elena – they'd all be paid and continue to be paid. The realization of what they'd all been doing for her suddenly dawned on her. All this time, they'd been working based on her promise that she'd take care of them when she could. They'd trusted her. What had they been thinking? They'd trusted her far more than she'd trusted herself. Without Jack Trumpet, she'd never be able to pay anybody anything. But, now, things were going to be different. If she had anything to say about it, the futures of her loyal staff would be secure. She suddenly felt like things were going to work; she suddenly felt like humming.

Marla patted her face with her $80 per ounce moisturizer, happy to realize that this would not, after all, be her last jar. She ran a brush through her frosted blonde pageboy and adjusted the black velvet headband and finished with a final pouf of hairspray before she fastened her mother's pearls around her neck. She was always studiously conscientious about preserving and protecting the one piece of her mother's jewelry that had escaped her father's dragnet when he was liquidating assets to pay his mill workers. She then stood back to admire the image of her black chiffon V-neck palazzo pantsuit. At least she still had one asset that had not been frozen.

6:01 p.m. The dinner was prepared; the hors d'oeuvres ready; Acumulada's brother Lorenzo was tending bar and Patrick would be downstairs. They'd have a quick drink together before the others arrived. His reaction to today's events would be interesting to say the least.

CAVIAR PIE

1 (8 oz.) container whipped cream	*½ cup. Finely chopped parsley*
Cheese	*1 (1 oz.) jar black caviar*
4 hard boiled eggs, peeled	*1 (4 oz.) jar red caviar*
5 finely chopped scallions	*3 Tb. Sour cream*

Mix cream cheese and sour cream until smooth. Spread evenly in serving platter. Cut eggs in halves and remove yolks. Chop yolks and whites separately. Mound black caviar in center of plate atop cream cheese mixture. Create concentric circles of: chopped egg yolks, then scallions, then red caviar, then egg whites and, lastly, parsley. Serve with assorted crackers.

CHAPTER 14

▼

The library was beginning to fill. Even though Maria Elena's cataracts were, in fact, fully ripe, she was able to pitch in and help her sister out. Sharp, clear vision is really not essential to taking guests' coats and umbrellas. While Maria Elena hung more fur in the hall closet than most Canadian trappers saw in a lifetime, Acumulada got a start on the real evening's work. She covered the room, creating figure eights weaving through the guests serving and clearing, serving and clearing. Acumulada never failed to remember who took four olives in their gin and who liked their Jameson's with ginger ale. Ilana Rubin and her harp took up an entire corner, but, unfortunately, her prodigious musical talent was wasted on this crowd. She could have broken into a medley of Metallica's all time greatest hits and no one would have noticed. Free booze is so much more interesting than harp music.

The conversations taking place around the room were a sophisticated version of can-you-top-this. Patrick, handsome in navy Armani and a perfectly cut custom made monogrammed shirt, listened intently as Florence and Everett Bainbridge described their most recent trip. Their favorite stop was the Amanpuri in Phuket Thailand where the ratio of staff to guest is 4 to 1. Florence adored the idea that it took a minimum of four to pick up and dispose of her never ending trail of dry cleaning plastic, tissue paper stuffing; thrown off shoes, crumpled magazines and *National Enquirers*, exercise clothes and half empty Tab cans. Was she recreating the Mom she never knew? She'd never know. Florence could, without the slightest effort, recount and rate the level of service on every cruise line or at every luxury hotel on the globe. She loved being serviced. She was particularly impressed with the elaborately paper-wrapped laundry at Amanpuri which was delivered to her suite in a silk lined wicker gift box topped with a fresh flower and compared their laundry delivery wrapping skills with that of staff at the Makaladi Private Game Reserve in South Africa or La Mamounia in Marrakesh. Patrick made a mental note to review and possibly upgrade the packaging of accessories that were bought in his Newbury Street store.

The usual people were telling the usual stories. Marla had heard them all before. As she greeted each guest, Marla realized she was, for the first time in a long time, genuinely glad to see each and every one of them. With a couple of possible exceptions. She realized it had been a long time since she'd felt this relaxed. It had to be because she could finally see the light at the end of her financial tunnel. This television thing could work out. Besides, no one would watch it anyway and, she'd still be paid.

Here they were, the little core of The Club, the membership committee. Everyone just back from the winter someplace. The Franklins had spent the winter in their house in Nevis; Walter and Addie had been boning up on Native American languages in New Mexico and Florence and Everett had been who knows where. Marla was one of the few people she knew who actually still stayed up here in the cold during the winter. But, the little nucleus had come out of hibernation to vote on whether or not to accept two new members – Fuller's bride-to-be and the Jack Trumpets.

Addie Coolidge, in fringed buckskin and a preponderance of feathers protruding from various points on her body, had found Pam and Fuller and had them blockaded against the Renoir in the hall.

"We took the Acela down last weekend and saw *Tosca* at the Met." She directed her next remark to Pam. "I know you're too young, darling, but are you familiar with Callas' *Tosca*?"

Callasasstosca?? Pam was not sure if she should risk disgracing herself completely by guessing that callasasstosca was some sort of dessert, musician or skin condition. Callasasstosca, callasasstosca. The Met. Wasn't the Met an art museum? Was it a painting? Maybe it was some special kind of cello like a violin or viola. Callasasstosca. Her eyes widened and her tongue tied. Was not knowing what Callasasstosca was enough of a reason for them to vote down her membership?

Her doe eyes implored Fuller.

And, he did not disappoint.

"We don't have a lot of time for opera, Mrs. Coolidge. When we're in New York, there's so much theatre to see. New exciting theatre. Fabulous concerts, daring new art. After we've seen all that's new, we'll go back and see a lot of those old things. I have a feeling they'll always be doing a *Tosca* somewhere in the world."

He squeezed Pam's elbow reassuringly. "Actually, Pam and I have heard Maria Callas as Tosca, not live, of course. With what they can do now digitally remastering, the CD's are sometimes even better than being there in person." He turned to Pam. "We listened to it in the car on the way up to Killington last Christmas. It was Callas' *Tosca"* without the guy snoring in the next seat." He grinned the handsome grin that Pam had fallen in love with. "Now, Mrs. Coolidge, tell me about this interesting costume you're wearing tonight."

"I'm not sure if you know or not, Fuller, but Walter and I have been returning to our roots. It was brought to our attention when the Pocahontas movie was released that the real story of Pocahontas varies somewhat from the movie. One thing that the movie does not mention is that Pocahontas and John Rolfe were the ancestors of the wife of Robert E. Lee, someone in the Clinton administration and the Coolidges of Boston. We've taken it upon ourselves to adopt the culture of our people and bring to public awareness our struggle as an oppressed minority by, among other things, the museum we're establishing."

Fuller wondered if Walter ever got a word in. The stone faced man, the man who actually was purportedly biologically descended from the Indian princess remained as silent as the cigar store variety while Addie continued.

"There's so much to do, now that I'm a career woman. People have no idea what it's like. People with these little silly cooking and candle dipping things that they do. They just have no idea what a real career means. I'm exhausted all the time. Just exhausted."

"She's exhausted." Walter *could* speak.

"Are you both Native American?" Pam asked innocently. "Back home in Albuquerque, we have just loads of Native Americans. That's just such a cute thing to call them", she giggled. "Native Americans. I'm real familiar with the way Native Americans do stuff."

Fuller smiled adoringly at his bride-to-be. "Maybe you and Addie could get together sometime and discuss a way you could help her out with the new museum. You'd be a great resource, hon."

"Think?"

"You'd be a great resource for anyone, anytime."

Little Pam seemed like a sweet enough girl Marla thought. Seemed educable, at least. Eventually, she'd be fine. Fuller would see to that. Addie Coolidge didn't throw her for a *complete* loop. But, where were the others? Addie and Walter's nominees. The Trumpets. The benefactors to Addie's Native American museum?

Then, there she was. From across a crowded room, Marla spotted her. The perfect, if disconnected features hovered beneath a bright carrot orange mane and above a garment of the oddest shade of violet Marla had ever seen. The pants were slit down the front from mid-thigh to the ankle. The shirt, if you could call it that, may as well have been painted on and painted on by a failed Picasso disciple. Swirling lines of sequins and irridized spandex created something that resembled a face which stretched across the woman's chest. Baroque pearls as big as moth balls hung across the whole vision. She clutched the arm of her escort adoringly. It took a moment for Marla to recognize Jack Trumpet with his clothes on, but yes, unmistakably, here he was. And here, hanging on his arm, was her future; here was her ticket out of the slippery slope heading to impoverished nobility; here was her co host; floating in on a bisected purple and orange cloud, here was Barbie Lee Trumpet.

"Darling, I'd like you to meet Marla Stone." Jack Trumpet was not an unattractive man if one had not recently been subjected to the sight of his hairless body, his nipples and his tiny hands. Dressed as he was tonight, some might actually consider him not unattractive.

"It's a pleasure to meet you, Mrs. Trumpet". Marla thought formality was the best course. She fully expected to be instructed to "call me Barbie Lee", but no such instructions were forthcoming.

"Delighted, I'm sure." Barbie's voice was startling. It was not a speaking voice one heard often. The words floated slowly up from her diaphragm and exited her mouth on a pouf of air. "My husband has informed me that you and I shall be collaborating together on a joint venture."

Marla hesitated. She hadn't actually agreed yet. Not formally. Not to him. Nothing was in writing yet. She could still back out. "We have talked briefly, yes."

"You'll enjoy it with pleasure I'm sure. When one is in the public eye performing, one can feel the feelings of love emanating from the audience." She clutched her scrawny bosom just about at the eyebrow of the face clinging to her skin. She could feel the rapture. "I feel it all the time. Feelings of love emanating from the audience. It is a most pleasant experience." She sucked in a gulp of air in order to expel the next line. "It will be a unique experience for you."

Unique? It wouldn't really be a *unique* experience for her. Maybe Marla hadn't felt feelings of love emanating from many audiences. Her actual audience exposure had been quite limited. In fact her only audiences had been her students and the tiny cadre of loyal readers of her newsletter. Once, Cheryl Frankenheimer had complimented her on her gold-leafing and stenciling techniques. Would that qualify as feelings of love emanating from the audience? Probably not. What about the time she demonstrated using spun sugar as a topping for an apple tart to her food presentation class? They seemed pleased. Was that feelings of love emanating from the audience? Or how about her little tip to always give the pasta a gentle twist as one puts it on the plate? People enjoyed that. But, perhaps this *could* be a new experience. Perhaps her association with Barbie Lee would open new doors for her – show her new ways of feeling love emanating from the audience. She touched the hand of her new co-host.

"I'm delighted to welcome you to our little neighborhood. Are you settled into the new house? I haven't seen that house for years, not since the Herricks lived there."

"I was just relating to Jack that the edifice requires a prodigious amount of reconstruction."

"Really?"

"I descended the stairs to the lower level this forenoon and ascertained that we have water or a different liquid leaking into our home. I presume that the water is entering from the ground area on the exterior of the outside."

Perhaps the woman had suffered an injury from having a dictionary fall on her head when she was a child.

"I'm awfully sorry to hear that. Perhaps I could offer you the names of some good repairmen in the area?" This was not the sort of cocktail chit chat Marla was accustomed to before dinner, but what could she do?

"You may not," came the reply, "I shan't be at home. I will be staying at a hotel this evening and shan't return to my home until the problem has been rectified. A member of my husband's staff shall be assigned the task. I am fearful that the concrete floor in the lower area may be permanently disfigured."

"If I may offer a suggestion, removing rust stains from concrete can be easily done by scrubbing the surface with a mixture of oxalic acid and water, using one pound of acid per gallon of water, being sure to add the acid to the water, not the water to the acid. Apply the mixture with a mop and wait three hours. Rinse with clean water, then scrub with a wire brush.

"I beg your pardon? Are you speaking to me?" The horrified look on Barbie's face caused Marla to take half a step back. It was not the look of feelings of love.

"Funny enough, my home repair and maintenance class was just working on a project where we researched various stain removal techniques. Rust from concrete was one of them. I daresay you'll be needing to do that once the water is pumped out."

"And, I daresay some member of my husband's staff will be overseeing the personnel to eradicate any stainage in my home, Mrs. Stone, but I am appreciative of your consideration." A breath. "Jackie, I gotta siddown." This sound was from a different person, a different planet. No more diaphragm floating. No more pouf of air. This voice came from a location no lower than the upper throat and made its way into the world via the perfectly formed nostrils.

"Please, don't let me keep you. Make yourself comfortable." Marla spoke directly to Barbie's back.

Marla watched her make her way across the marble foyer and noticed gleefully, ashamed of her glee, but gleeful nonetheless that Barbie's flopping backless Versace mules were identical to those Acumulada had been wearing during her *Guiding Light* break this morning.

Marla took a step back and admired her beautiful room filled with her friends and the rest of them. She had arranged a lovely evening. The rain was falling steadily and often heavily, but thank God and thank Acumulada's prayers, it wasn't snow. Everything was going smoothly. The rhythmic yet subtle throb of the sump pump in the basement that only Marla was aware of was just enough reassurance that all mechanical systems in the house were operating. All of the personalities in the house were also operational: Florence and Everett were kvetching to the Franklins about the quality of the Eggs Florentine in Florence; Walter and Addie had Pam and Fuller pinned in the corner grilling the poor little cheerleader on her knowledge of the fine arts and, Patrick, bless his heart, had assumed the task of entertaining the Trumpets. The evening was going well.

Marla had dismissed Ilana for the evening and Guido and Lorenzo both insisted on driving her home. Guido would return later to retrieve the cars from Ledge's crazy garage. Marla almost felt almost giddy as she walked over to the French doors to the dining room. She could survive 13 weeks with Barbie Lee. And, after that, she would continue on her own without a "co-host". She was sure viewers would like her. Her students all did, her readers all did. At least she thought they did. Thirteen weeks was nothing in the whole scheme of things, as long as it meant financial freedom for her.

She stood at her place at the head of her dining table and surveyed her handiwork. The table had long ago been set, but she just wanted to be sure that the single Phaleonopsus placed beside each place card was angled correctly. She couldn't put her finger on it, but something was amiss. The candles were perfectly erect and all the same height; the shell pink Madeira cloth hung perfectly; no specks of anything marred the Lenox china and Tiffany silver. It must just be a case of stage fright. This was, after all, a significant evening for her. This was to be the last time she would see any of these people as simply the teacher of lifestyle classes in her home and writer, editor and publisher of the *Stone Home Improvement Trust*. After tonight, things were going to be very different.

It was time to formally welcome her guests. Marla took a deep breath and threw open the double doors and swept into the library.

"Good evening, ladies and gentlemen. May I have your attention." The chatter was immediately hushed. Marla's classroom technique was not wasted on the occupants of her library. "I'd like to extend a gracious Club welcome to you all and to our very special guests this evening. As you know, the membership committee will be voting later tonight on two new applications. Miss Pamela Yewlah, who is being proposed by Fuller Arden." She smiled at the handsome young man she'd known since his birth. She felt almost as close to Fuller as she did to Charles and Billy, sometimes even more so. "And, Mr. and Mrs. Jack Trumpet. Jack and Barbie Lee Trumpet." Marla nodded in the general direction of the brightly clothed couple and smiled a very different smile than the one she'd bestowed on Fuller and Pam. Please enjoy the hors d'oeuvres and enjoy getting to know our new applicants until we serve dinner in", she glanced at her watch "just about an hour."

Patrick was at her side. "They don't seem that bad."

I suppose I'll get used to them. A person can get used to pretty much anything, isn't that so? Starvation, solitary confinement, flying coach? I'll be OK. I'm actually feeling a little better about the prospects. Besides, it's only 13 weeks."

"It had better be more than 13 weeks if you expect to make any money on this." He patted the pocket where he usually kept his cell phone. "Old Mr. Young called this afternoon. He tried to reach you."

"Patrick, I hope you didn't bring one of those contraptions into this house."

"Don't worry, babe." He opened his jacket to reveal his empty pocket. "I'm clean. Force of habit, couldn't help it, auto reflex. The contraption is safely locked up in the car. But, babe, you have to understand, that's what old Mr. Young called about. There's not much money for you during the first 13 weeks of the run. If this show isn't renewed after the first 13 weeks, then you're back to square one, nowheresville, zero, zilch, nada. You need to look at the long term, the big picture, the whole enchilada, the whole ball of wax, the whole nine yards."

Patrick had run out of synonyms.

"I *am* thinking of the long term. But, I only have to have my co-host for the first 13 weeks. After that, I'll continue it alone. It's only for 13 weeks that I have to contend with her." She paused. "Isn't that the way the contract is written?"

"Actually no." Patrick was going to explain the terms to a particularly slow child. "The initial term is for 13 weeks. At the end of the initial 13 weeks, the contract is renewable, but it's only renewable by her, not by you."

"What are you saying?" Marla almost whispered. "Are you saying that if the people like me and I want to continue doing the show, I can only do it if I do it with her? Is that it?"

"That's pretty much it. But, once you've established yourself and have a following and have spread your wings and earned your stripes and proven your mettle, you'll be in a stronger position to negotiate, more like the catbird seat. Old Mr. Young can take another look, take another shot at it, revisit the contract then."

"If the show's a success, she'll never want to get out."

Acumulada appeared at Marla's elbow from out of nowhere balancing the house intercom receiver in one hand and a tray of champagne glasses in the other. "Missus, I'm sorry to interrupt, but somebody's outside, - the crazy lady."

Marla scanned her inventory of acquaintances and could easily pick out two or three dozen who might fit that description.

"The crazy lady, Missus, the one with the red face who makes the lights in the pictures."

"Oh, she said she thought she'd try to make it. Do show her in, Acumulada."

"She's here, Missus". Acumulada handed Marla the phone. Marla was confused.

"Lulu, is that you darling?"

"I'm outside your front door. And, it's raining cats and dogs and blowing like a son-of-a-bitch. Who ever heard of this kind of weather this time of year. I'm freezing. Listen, Marla, send someone down to let me in. There's no one out here."

"Darling, the meeting was called for six. We're all already here. There's no reason for Guido to stay, now is there?"

"Can't trust any of them. They just dash out at the stroke of five".

"It was the stroke of six and, really, there was no reason for him to stay. Frankly, Lulu, we didn't expect you". Marla was beginning to let her impatience show.

"Marla, I told you I'd try. I said I'd try. Now, do you think you can send someone down?"

"Don't be silly, Of course, darling. I'll let you in myself. Jolly glad you're going to be able to join us," Marla said.

"Jolly glad? What's wrong?" Lulu had known Marla for a very long time.

"Oh, nothing, everything. I'll come straight away to open the door." She turned to Acumulada. "Let's set a place for our dear Lulu."

"It's done, Missus." As the golden tooth flickered in the candlelight, it dawned on Marla what had bothered her about the table settings. She and Patrick were on either end. Could it have been five on one side, six on the other. Was that it?

CHAPTER 15

▼

Marla was a firm believer in placecards. Not only did they add a nice vertical dimension to a topographically boring table setting (they didn't call it flatware for nothing), they really did succeed in easing the attendant bedlam as alcohol-lubricated guests descended on the dining table en masse. For this group tonight, however, bedlam was the guest of honor. People were all over the table, trying to sit in someone else's seat, examining and re-examining the seating plan, totally disregarding the beautifully calligraphed placecards. There was so much up and down, seat swapping and scuffling, one would have thought Marla had surprised them with a game of musical chairs before dinner.

Walter Coolidge absolutely refused to wear his reading glasses. It was as if the two-toned goatee of black in the middle sandwiched by two strips of white up to his sideburns would cause anyone to mistake him for a teenager. He insisted that the card he clutched in his hand which was boldly inscribed "Lucretia" marked his place. Sometimes, Marla just couldn't understand what people were thinking. She would never seat a husband and wife next to one another and Lucretia's card was right beside Fuller's down at Patrick's end of the table. Walter should have known if only he'd wear those damn glasses.

Patrick had heard a curious little factoid recently and although he'd already shared it with everyone within earshot, felt it would be a good distraction to use to get Walter to his assigned seat.

"Hey, Walt, do you know where the WGBH broadcast tower is?"

"I heard you say it earlier, but … can't say …" Walter's bone dry martinis had kicked in quite a while ago.

"The top of Great Blue Hill. GBH. Get it?" Patrick loved this. The fact that Walter Coolidge's family foundation had given quite a few bucks to the station over the years and old Walter had never heard about the derivation of the call letters pleased Patrick no end. He got Walter settled in his seat and headed down to take his place at the end of the table opposite Marla. He passed Fuller. "Hey Full, do you know where the GBH tower is?"

Fuller couldn't imagine why he wanted to know. Had someone misplaced it? "Why, it's at the top of Great Blue Hill, isn't it?" Patrick found Fuller to be quite annoying.

Poor little Pam. She clutched her place card and flashed her eyes from Fuller to the card, from the card to Fuller. She was beside herself that she and her beloved were to be separated for the duration of the meal. With the pining farewell, one might have thought Fuller was leaving for 11 months in Da Nang rather than two hours 15 feet away. The girl was a mess. Marla certainly did not approve of eavesdropping, but could hardly help hearing Pam's protestations. If this little cheerleader had any real aspirations of becoming Mrs. Fuller Arden and, as such, assuming her place as a full voting member of The Club, with all its attendant social responsibilities, she'd better get used to the idea of being dinner partner to the head of a major corporation. She'd better learn to feel comfortable being on her own to socialize and entertain heads of state, philanthropists, full professors and blubbery little pink nosed Buddhas who insist that you sit "just a little closer" so you can hear the punch line of their dirty joke. Pam was just making far too much of the fact that Jack Trumpet was CEO of a company; that he was frequently interviewed by the *Wall Street Journal*; that he'd appeared on television. It wouldn't be too long before Pam and everyone else in this room would have to become accustomed to getting together with someone who appeared on television on a very regular basis; with someone people on the street would recognize far more easily than a face whose black and white image showed up from time to time in a newspaper; with someone who had their own daily lifestyle show. This little girl, this little Pam, this little girl from Abilene or Albuquerque or wherever it was, would just have to get a grip on herself. Maybe Marla could be able to get her alone and slap some sense into her, figuratively, of course. If Marla had had a daughter, these were the kinds of valuable life lessons that she would have been taught. The daughter of Marla Stone would have manners, would have composure, would know how to conduct herself under any conditions. That's what manners were for. Manners allowed one to be comfortable or at least appear comfortable under virtually any circumstances. Pity that from what Fuller had told her, Pam had not had the benefit of a mother to teach her life's important lessons.

Prior to a large gathering, Marla always opened a few windows and cooled a room off. Fresh, clean air made a room a lot more comfortable. With the storm raging outside and building up greater and greater intensity, an open window tonight was out of the question. The unreliable old creaky central air had to be turned on to try to lower the room's temperature to a level Marla felt would be comfortable for her guests. The air would have to be unfreshened. She had, long ago, worked it out. She'd figured how cool it should be to be able to absorb the body heat of x number of diners. She never made it too cold; it was always just subtly *refreshing* to walk into Marla Stone's dining room. The temperature was perfectly comfortable for everyone, everyone except Lucretia.

Lucretia Franklin wound her apricot Pashmina more tightly around her sequined tank top. The sequined tank top was one she'd purchased in the children's department of a dance costume shop. Lucretia needed fewer sequins than most to cover her 87 pounds and resented paying the same for her clothes as the ample size 16's and up among her acquaintance. She'd paid full price for her Pashmina, but at least she used the full volume of it and used it to its best advantage – wrapped like a shroud around her bony shoulders for warmth. There was never enough cashmere or mink to warm Lucretia. She needed the warmth of the sun to tan her leathery skin on the outside and the warmth of a burning cigarette to heat up the inside. She was, indeed, a frigid woman. She was not listening to Patrick who was doing his best to be entertaining. He was trying to tell a joke he'd read on the Internet and it was not translating well. It had something to do with a pizza being able to get to your house faster than an ambulance, but the joke was just not working. It didn't matter because no one was really listening to him, so he tried that old where's the WGBH tower poll. No takers. Poor Patrick.

Lucretia leaned on her Pashmina padded bony elbow and regarded her husband a few seats away. He was also telling a joke – one he'd heard 30 years ago. The old fool with this close to making Fuller's little lady blush scarlet. For all of his faults, Dr. Elmore Franklin could tell a joke. The one thing he couldn't do was follow his destiny; obey fate. He was supposed to be dead; she was supposed to be a widow. Elmore Franklin had been scheduled to die at age 52, twelve long years ago. His death had been predicted. A very well regarded psychic -one who's called in by police on cold cases, no fly-by-night scam artist - had told Lucretia to prepare. And so, she did. The man had more insurance on his life than Betty Grable had had on her legs. Lucretia sold her jewelry, liquidated her stock portfolio, scraped together every dime she had to buy a $200 million policy on her husband's life and just quietly waited. One year, two. A third year of those outrageous premiums. But, it had to be done. And, he was starting to look a little tired. She never mentioned the psychic's prediction nor his extraordinary insurance coverage.

Then, the unthinkable. Three days before his 52nd birthday, he attended a medical conference on laser hair removal in Cincinnati. Rather than come directly home and spend his birthday with the family (he knew Lucretia wouldn't mind) he decided to stay on one extra day and take advantage of the invitation of Conglomotron and check out their laser manufacturing plant in Wildwood, Ohio. Thank God he did. The DC-10 he was booked on the day earlier exploded on take off. No survivors. If he had been on that plane ... Needless to say, Lucretia was shocked. Now, here he was, sitting at the same table as the man whose company, whose hair removal laser, had been responsible for saving his life. He couldn't wait to go over and shake Jack Trumpet's hand. Lucretia felt quite differently.

The little Albuquerque cheerleader much preferred Dr. Franklin's dodging-the-bullet-second-chance-at-life story to his earlier joke about the nun and the golfer which she wasn't sure she understood anyway.

Lucretia had heard the second chance at life story probably four or five thousand times and, by now, could recite it verbatim, including the guffaws and elongated pauses. The luck of meeting Jack Trumpet at that conference; the unidentifiable prescience that this hair removal laser was something that would be important to his life; the wonder of a universe where all of these things were preordained. The story was always the same. Lucretia prepared herself to hear Elmore tell Pam the story of the time he met Ted Williams after a Red Sox game and then about the time Eleanor Roosevelt addressed him by name. That was the expected sequence. Elmore had not always been boring, but, unfortunately, he should have died when he was supposed to. God had only allotted Elmore 52 years worth of stories. From then on, he had to repeat the same ones over and over. Just like this joke he'd just tried to tell Pam.

Lucretia clamped her teeth down on the plastic cigarette she always carried. Marla, like everyone else in this godawful country, would never permit noxious fumes to be exhaled in her home. While she daydreamed about the benefits of living in Korea or some other place where people could actually smoke when they wanted to, she couldn't help but notice the drama that was unfolding down at Marla's end of the table. She watched the man whose hair removal laser was responsible for her life being turned topsy turvy. She watched as he and his little woman, standing behind his assigned seat, prepared to duke it out, whispering yells to one another behind Lulu's and Florence's back as if they were not there.

"I'm not sitting there, Jack. I don't know how you can expect me to sit there."

"Come on, sweetheart. It's right next to Patrick. It's the seat of honor. The best seat at the table."

"Do you see where the light is? I can't sit there." The flaming red hair could not be contained.

"It's only candlelight, sweetheart.

"I can see that it's candlelight, Jackie. Do I look stupid or what? I can see that it's candlelight. But, it's light; it casts shadows; it's coming from my right; I'm not sitting here. I just can't. How many times can I say the same thing to you? Are you listening? I'm not sitting here. Can you hear me? Nod if you can hear me."

"Sweetheart, you face looks fine. I don't know what you're worried about."

"The implant on the right side is still too high. It hasn't settled down yet. It's not settled. I think it's still swollen. Doesn't it look swollen? I'm unable to sit here, Jack. There is too much light."

She folded her arms across her Picasso chest and spun away from her husband, exposing a full view of the settled non-swollen, perfectly smooth cheek implant on the left side of her face. She stamped her Versace shod feet for emphasis. The petulant nine-year old had spoken. "I have to go home now. We were supposed to have sushi tonight. They're probably serving some gross food anyway. These people always do. Some kind of white carbs."

✳   ✳   ✳   ✳

Macaroni & Cheese

½ *lb. Macaroni cooked*   10 *Tbsps. butter*

1 ½ *cups hot milk*   1 ½ *cups cheddar cheese, shredded*

salt and pepper

Arrange macaroni, cheese and butter in alternating layers in a buttered baking dish. Season with salt and pepper. Add hot milk and top with more cheese. Bake at 350 for 25 minutes or until cheese is melted and bubbly.

"Sweetheart, what can we do? We're guests here." With a shrug he turned to look to Marla, his eyes begging for her help.

"I say, is everything alright over here?" Marla spoke to Barbie Lee's back. She was not turning around. Not yet, anyway.

Jack was apologetic. "It's nothing. Just the seats. I hate to ask and wouldn't ordinarily. It's just that …" His voice trailed off.

Barbie Lee had finally deigned to turn around. She inhaled deeply, paused and floated her request on the cloud of exhaled carbon dioxide. "I desire a permutation in my seating accommodations."

"Why certainly, of course, Mrs. Trumpet. Anything to make my guests more comfortable." Marla was quite horrified. "Is it the chair? The window? Is your glass chipped? Do you need a pillow? Anything I can do …"

What was wrong? This ridiculous little creature was not the only one who was uncomfortable. Something was happening. The sub-audible noise that had reassured Marla all evening was now more than sub-audible; it was inaudible. The rumble under the floor that always made her feel as though she were on a cruise ship wasn't there. The sump pump in the cellar had stopped. The snow which Acumulada had predicted had, blessedly, stopped. In its place though came the rain. Rain, incessant, pouring, torrential and it showed no signs of letting up. Marla was more than familiar with the water table on her little island in Massachusetts Bay. Without her sump pumps clanging, her cellar could take on water in a matter of hours. Depending on the saturation of the land, it could be a matter of minutes. There had been an unusually heavy snowfall this past winter; the rivers and reservoirs were all lapping over their banks, to say nothing of the Atlantic Ocean. More water was not something they needed this year.

Marla forced herself to focus on the pouty little face. Another gulp of air and another sentence floated between collagened lips. "I'll acquire the assignment originally assigned to my husband. Thanks a lot."

What had she just said? It took a few moments for Marla to process her request. It suddenly registered and Marla picked up the cards which marked the places of each of the Trumpets. "Don't even hesitate. It is done. Your wish is my command." At least she wasn't asking to check out the French drains in the cellar. "I daresay Patrick was looking forward to having you all to himself down there, but if it makes you feel better to change seats, it is done. There is absolutely no question."

With a rustle of spandex brushing cashmere, Mr. and Mrs. Jack Trumpet dosey-doed around one another to take their newly assigned seats.

Marla took a sip from her water glass. Would this horrible evening ever be over? Would it ever begin? All she wanted to do was to have this behind her. What was suddenly behind her though, was Acumulada followed by a very large, very angry, very Black man.

"I'm sorry, missus. I thought he was invited. He said he wanted the man with the wig."

Fuller was on his feet. "What is the meaning of this?"

Jack Trumpet slouched deep into himself and managed to become partially concealed behind Florence Bainbridge. He ran his fingers through the luxuriant growth on the top of his head and whispered to Florence. "This is not a wig. This is my own. Now."

Florence couldn't handle violence of any kind and began to experience a flashback of her fling with Ledge (particularly the evening he was found in the trunk of her Bentley) and was rendered speechless.

"Where is he? I was acquitted. He can't do this to an acquitted man. Where is he?" P.D. Quinn roared. "That little snake, I'll kill him. I did a good job for him. He can't just fire me. I was acquitted."

In the time it took for Quinn to scan the table and locate the crouching Trumpet, Fuller had leapt across the table and thrown his young athletic kay-aker's body against the massive but arthritic football player. Quinn was blind-sided. It took him too long to react and he was down. Fuller Arden, pink cheeks flushed with the thrill of a real tackle, demanded in righteous indignation, "Again, pal, what the hell's going on here?" He had really decked and was really accosting a real black guy. Wow.

"It's him, the guy with the wig."

All eyes turned to the man on the floor behind Florence. "This guy's crazy. It was business. I was well within my legal rights to terminate. I don't need to have a *spokesman* who's accused of murdering his wife. And with one of our golf clubs, no less. If you'd read the fine print, you'd see that I had every right to terminate."

"I'm an acquitted man. I did a good job for your motherfuckin' company." Quinn croaked out his response. With Fuller's size 13 penny loafers on his throat, speech was difficult.

"I don't give a shit. You were accused. I don't need that. I don't need that kind of publicity. My company has an image to protect."

Marla was suddenly her serene highness. "Gentlemen, gentlemen. Can't we postpone this discussion until after dinner? Fuller, please?" She turned to the man pinned on her dining room floor. "Mr. Quinn, isn't it? I've seen you on the telly. How do you do?"

"It's a pleasure. Sorry for the little misunderstanding, Ma'am."

"I'm sure you are. Now, Mr. Quinn, or may I call you Petey. I say, can I invite you to join us for dinner? Old Mr. Young should be along straight away".

"Yeah, sure and, it's P.D., two letters, p and d. Get it? P.D."

"Of course. Fuller, darling, would you please release Mr. Quinn."

Trumpet was outraged. "You can't invite him to stay. This man is a criminal."

"I was acquitted."

The voice of reason spoke. "This man is already soaked to the skin. Take a look out the window, Mr. Trumpet. You may not have noticed it, but since we've sat down, this little rain we were having has turned into a gale, a hurricane, a tsunami. We couldn't send anyone out in this."

Barbie Lee offered her two cents worth. "Maybe we should let him remain. He is Black, after all and the precipitation is precipitous."

Jack was outgunned. He had no strength to resist. Barbie Lee wanted him to stay. Marla wanted him to stay. Even Patrick had thrown in on the stay side. What could he do? "What time is old Mr. Young getting here? He'll be able to explain the legalese to you, Quinn, and you'll see that I was well within my rights to terminate."

Quinn glared at Trumpet. Trumpet glared at Quinn. Marla could feel a migraine coming on. "Oh, bloody hell. Let's just wait for old Mr. Young, shall we? We're all civilized adults here. We can't let this little difference of opinion ruin everyone's evening." She turned to Acumulada. "We can set another place for." She stopped midsentence as Acumulada walked to the table carrying a place setting of China and silver in one hand and a frosty Martini glass in the other.

"I hope that's a Grey Goose and I hope it's for me."

"Si, missus. And the Chinaman's powder."

"Jolly good show."

CHAPTER 16

▼

Could it be possible that the dinner party had finally settled into some semblance of normalcy? The migraine that had been threatening hadn't really had a chance to take over. Marla might just escape without having to resort to dumping the packet of Mr. Woo's herbs into her teacup and drinking that in lieu of the fabulous meal she'd prepared. Most of the guests seemed to be trying to behave. The unannounced arrival of a homicidal, albeit acquitted black man who had walked all the way across the bridge from town in the pouring rain had perhaps shaken them up sufficiently to put things into perspective. Or perhaps the alcohol had simply worn off. Elmore Franklin had abandoned his stand up comedy act for his audience of one; while Fuller relaxed, smug in the knowledge of his success in downing the big guy. He was the hunter. He was the man. And, later tonight, Pam would show her appreciation the way only Pam could. Florence and Everett only touched on their litany of complaints about some five-star hotel in Kuala Lumpur. Walter had settled in to a deadening dissertation about the future of the educated classes. He'd read an alarming statistic. High school drop outs begin to reproduce at around age 15; whereas, for college educated women, the average age was 30. According to his figures, eventually an entire generation of college educated intelligentsia would be lost to the unchained spawning of the great unwashed. Pam just knew Walter Coolidge could see the flush in her face at the mention of the very age her mother had been when Pam had been born. But, aside from this little aside, things could be a lot worse. Even Addie had, for the moment at least, stopped complaining about how hard she worked. All was right with the world. Or, was it?

Marla nodded to Patrick down at the other end of the table. He was trying his best with Lucretia, but it was no use. Patrick had a little too much time on his hands and he'd figured out that Vicks Nyquil at $8.35 for a 6 oz. bottle, sold for $178.13 per gallon and Pepto Bismol, at $3.85 for a 4 oz. bottle came to $123.20 per gallon. And, weren't we all glad our cars didn't run on Nyquil. Har har. Lucretia was more interested in sucking on her plastic cigarette and examining her face for any enlarged pores in the 5x magnifying mirror that she always carried than she was in Patrick's efforts to amaze. She only glanced at him with bored half opened eyes and sighed. Patrick needed to be done with his chit chat. It was time for him to get to work. It was time for him to propose a toast to the guests and to his hostess and officially begin the meal. If the meal ever got started, it could eventually be *over*.

Patrick rose and lifted his glass. It was his job to open the proceedings, kick things off; get things underway; jump start the engine; get the show on the road. Marla always wanted him to do this. Propose a toast to the guests and to her; set the tone for the evening. It was his pleasure, he was happy to do it. He was glad to; he was there for her. It was just that, maybe someday he could be more in her life than escort and toastmaster. Maybe someday, the guests would be proposing a toast to him and Marla, the happy couple. But, she'd been burned. That damn Ledge. OK. He'd do it. He'd prove to her that he wasn't like Ledge, that she could rely on him, that he could be counted on, that he was a man of his word, a stand up guy.

Patrick stood up. "Ladies and gentlemen, may I have your attention, please."

The magpies stopped chattering. Something else stopped also, Marla was sure of it. The rumbling thump of the pump had stopped. No sound, no vibration from the floor. Marla listened carefully. During the little scuffle with P.D. Quinn, she had thought it might have stopped. Now she was sure. She was not listening to Patrick's prattle. She was listening to the unrelenting silence coming up from the floor and the unrelenting torrent pouring down on the roof. The rain was coming down in sheets, borne on the wind straight off the ocean. Unlike the pumps, the rain had not stopped; it had not let up one bit. If anything, it was raining harder now than when the guests had arrived. Just let the evening be over, she prayed. I'll deal with whatever is happening in the cellar, with the sloshing flood that she was sure was down there once everyone leaves.

Every eye turned to Patrick's handsome face. If he weren't so stupid, Marla could probably grow to actually like him.

"I'd like to invite you to join me in a toast, a salute, a tribute to all of our guests this evening. Old friends and new."

Marla couldn't listen to this. She was calculating. All the rain that had fallen tonight, mixed with all the snow that had fallen yesterday that mixed with last winter's snow that was now melted and clogging the gutters and storm drains – all this water was rushing into her cellar, percolating up from the ground heading directly for her electrical panel. She could feel it. She could almost hear it flowing. Without the constant rumble of the pump to occupy her ear, a channel was available to fill with the imagined sounds of water flowing, coursing, rushing directly into her cellar.

"A special Club welcome, howdy, greeting and salutation to our new prospective members."

The damn pumps. Why hadn't she had them serviced? All they needed was to be cleaned out and lubricated, the intakes flushed and the floats replaced. Acumulada had reminded her to call. But, no. She'd been too busy. She'd barely found the time to go to that spirituality retreat where she tried to journey to the spirit realms the Tibetans call bardos to free herself of unwanted spirit attachments. She needed to finish the most recent installment of her history of Hammerston, to say nothing of dealing with her murdered ex and his ubiquitous spirit. And, besides, not too many people around here realized it, but going broke took up a fair amount of time. But, nevertheless, she should have done it. She shouldn't have gambled on something so important as sump pumps.

"Mr. and Mrs. Jack Trumpet. Jack and his lovely wife Bobbie."

Barbie Lee. Barbie Lee. Why couldn't anyone get that woman's name right. Marla nervously fingered the intricately wrapped paper package in her pocket. Her left eye was beginning to twitch. The next step in her migraine sequence was a steady throb. After that, her vision would become cloudy and once a headache got that far, she'd be down for days. She couldn't afford to be down for days. She had things to do. If she took Mr. Woo's herbs now, she could possibly be asleep before dessert. Maybe half now just to keep the migraine at bay and the other half as people were leaving. That could work. She hadn't had that much to drink.

"And to Pam Yewlah"

Pam's cheeks turned a deeper shade of pink. Deeper than mere blushing. Could it be that she was headed for a future of high coloring followed by a flaming face like poor Lulu? For Fuller's sake, Marla hoped not.

"As you probably all know, Pam and our own Fuller Arden have decided to tie the knot, jump the broomsticks, take the plunge." Patrick grinned. He was pretty. But not pretty enough.

Marla sipped on the concoction she'd created in the teacup of hot water Acumulada had placed in front of her. Her left eye continued its independent boogaloo. Maybe half wasn't going to be enough. It certainly wouldn't be enough if Patrick didn't get on with it. At this rate, they'd be here all night.

"And to our lovely hostess". Marla half-smiled serenely. She was Grace Kelly's serene highness coupled with Nancy Reagan's insincere lowness. Let's move it along, Patrick.

"Tonight is a special night for our little Marla. She's too modest to make the announcement herself, but, as of tomorrow morning, Marla Stone will be a member of Jack Trumpet's team. She's agreed to co-host a lifestyle show with none other than the lovely Bobbie Lee."

Barbie Lee.

"Let's all raise our glasses and say L'chaim".

CHAPTER 17

▼

"Hear Hear. Hear Hear. Marvelous, marvelous". The clinking of the Baccarat created the first pleasant sound Marla had heard all evening. The announcement that Marla and Barbie Lee would be joining forces on a television show came as no surprise to anyone. Word had spread throughout the cocktail hour to those who were sufficiently out of the loop not to have heard the news this afternoon. For propriety's sake, everyone feigned surprise. Everyone including old Mr. Young. What was he doing here already? He wasn't due for hours. Had it been that long? Had he already finished his dinner with the Bodines? What time was it? Was it already time to start the meeting? Marla instinctively looked at her wrist. Nothing. Where was her mind? The gold Cartier watch she'd been wearing that afternoon was sitting on her dressing table where she'd left it. Without a watch she had absolutely no conception of time. The time that passed could have been minutes; could have been hours. It was a function of age. She was sure of it.

The gazpacho had been set before each guest. That was a clear signal that the meal would thankfully, begin soon. That awful harpist had long finished playing, and had gone home, but not before Acumulada had offered to give her dinner in the kitchen with the rest of the help. Patrick had finally finished his soliloquy and, very soon the intended recipients would be trying the pork tenderloin (if Ilana had left any). Mr. Woo's herbs would soon be kicking in and Marla could enjoy or at least appear to enjoy the rest of the evening.

*　　*　　*　　*

PORK TENDERLOIN

3 lb. Boneless pork loin　　　　　*2 Tablespoons softened butter*

1 teaspoon mustard powder　　　　*1 ¼ teaspoon ground ginger*

½ teaspoon garlic powder　　　　*1 ¼ cup soy sauce*

¾ cup red wine　　　　　　　　*2 Tablespoons cornstarch*

salt and pepper

Combine butter, mustard powder, ginger, garlic powder, soy sauce and wine. Cut small slits in pork roast. Spread marinade over roast and marinate 1 – 2 hours. Roast 30 minutes at 450; remove from oven and let stand for 30 minutes. Return to oven and roast at 325 an additional 30 minutes until internal temperature reads 170. Sauce: Drain juices from roasting pan into a saucepan. Dissolve cornstarch in ¼ cup water. Combine dissolved cornstarch with pan juices. Boil 1 minute, stirring constantly. Serve sauce with roast.

No. What was that? From the cellar. A thud. A rumble. A whirr. A spark. A crash. Flicker. Darkness. Blackness. The toasting magpies started in earnest. One would think none of them had ever seen a power failure. Why, if one lived in California, these things happened all the time. But, here they were, all adults, all teetering on the brink of hysteria over a silly little power failure.

"Friends, friends. Please, remain calm. It's just the storm. I'm sure the power will be back any minute. We have plenty of candlelight and our meal has been prepared. Let's enjoy our little adventure."

If it were not for her certainty about the devastation and destruction that was going on in the environs of her electric panel, Marla would actually have been able to enjoy the lovely flickering of the hand dipped tapers illuminating the table.

"Acumulada, dear, be a love and help me get some more candles from the chest in the hall. Let's use the hand rolled beeswax, not the dipped. In the natural, not white. Those will look so lovely with the pink cloth. And, also, darling, could you bring a couple of torches from the kitchen hall. You and I can find our way in the dark." Marla was the soul of calm while everyone around her was falling apart. She appeared to thrive on chaos. It was just her stomach lining that didn't.

"Torches? Missus, I don't think big flames like that is good near the drapes."

"Not flaming torches, darling", she smiled. "American flashlights."

"Si, si. Lo siento. Oh, dio mio" She made the sign of the cross. "This used to happen in Lindo Labio. It is a bad omen".

"It's not an omen, luv, it's just a power failure."

In a twinkling, they were back, laden with more candles, candleholders, oil lamps of every description, but neither torches nor flashlights. The room was bedlam. Marla took charge. "Ladies and gentlemen, let's be calm. Let's not over-react. This is just a little power failure. We'll be fine. Our lovely dinner is prepared. We can enjoy it by candle oh-my-god." She saw with horror what her guests had uncovered while she was gone. The bright orange hair of her future cohost spilling from her soup plate onto the Madeira cloth. "What's wrong with her?"

Patrick and Dr. Franklin were at her elbow. "I'm afraid she's dead."

✱   ✱   ✱   ✱

GAZPACHO

3 cloves garlic	*3 pounds tomatoes*
2 cucumbers	*1 green pepper*
1 Bermuda onion	*2 cups iced tomato juice*
1/3 cup olive oil	*3 Tablespoons vinegar*
salt and pepper	*½ teaspoon Tabasco*
chopped cilantro to taste	

Chop, peel and seed the tomatoes and cucumbers. Add the finely chopped garlic. Chop the onion and green pepper. Add to mix. Add tomato juice. Add olive oil and seasonings, cover and chill several hours. Serve in chilled bowls with a cube of frozen tomato juice in each bowl.

Dead. Dead. How could she be dead? What happened? In the dark, Pam hugged Lucretia Franklin; Florence Bainbridge embraced Fuller and Addie; and Lulu Noone clung to P.D. Quinn. Odd bedfellows. All of them were suddenly silent. All in pairs or triads with the exception of Mr. Jack Trumpet who stood impassively over his dead wife. He appeared to be in a state of shock.

Elmore Franklin and Patrick the blind man took charge. "Ladies and gentlemen," Patrick was still in his public speaking mode. He assumed the role of mouthpiece. "We seem to have a situation here. If I may make a request, if you would be good enough, if you could see your way clear, would you all please retire to the library? It would probably be best to clear the immediate area around the situation. Investigative personnel might find it, well, we wouldn't want to contaminate the area with DNA from everyone in the room."

Fuller tapped into his brief military experience and managed to shepherd the rubber necking guests out of the room. "Let's take a couple of these oil lamps with us. There are no lights in there either, folks." Marla, Acumulada, Patrick and Dr. Franklin were left with the corpse and the grieving husband.

"DNA!! What was he saying? Did he actually think she was murdered?" Marla choked.

"My wife was in perfect health." Jack Trumpet was dispassionate. "She's never been sick a day in her life. I can only suspect foul play."

Foul play? Was the man actually suggesting that this little idiot had actually been murdered in her house? In her house!?

"Mr. Trumpet, just a minute. What are you saying?"

"What I'm saying, Mrs. Stone, is that my dear wife was in perfect health when we arrived here tonight and now, she's dead. I can only assume one thing."

"She may be dead, Mr. Trumpet, but murdered? Perhaps she suffered a heart attack or a stroke or a ..." Marla's medical vocabulary was quite limited unless she were describing the various acupuncture medians of the body or the colorations of the internal heat conditions Mr. Woo observed on her tongue.

"My wife was murdered, Mrs. Stone. Dr. Franklin here confirms it."

"Oh, Missus, are you sure she's dead?" Acumulada's golden tooth flickered in the candlelight.

"Acumulada, don't start. I think Dr. Franklin knows the difference between alive and dead. He said the woman's dead."

"When Prince Richard wanted to trick Prince Edmond into releasing Princess Cassie from the tower prison, he took some drugs that made him look dead."

"Acumulada, the *Guiding Light* and it's characters are not real. You've got to remember that. Let's just listen to Dr. Franklin."

"Ms. Candelaria is quite correct, Marla. There are drugs that in some very few patients repress respiration and heart beat sufficiently so that the patient appears dead, but it is very unusual. No. I'm afraid Mrs. Trumpet is quite dead. And, I'm afraid that it was not a heart attack, nor a seizure of any type. Mrs. Trumpet was poisoned.

"In my house!! On my food!! This can't be." Death was one thing. Improperly prepared food was quite another matter.

"It was not your food, per se, dear." Dr. Franklin tried his best to be calming. "But, if you can, please come close to the body. You'll detect the clear scent of burned almonds. That scent is definitely characteristic of cyanide poisoning."

"Cyanide!"

      ✳   ✳   ✳   ✳

ALMOND COOKIES

2/3 cup butter	*2/3 cup sugar*
1 teaspoon salt	*1 teaspoon baking soda*
1 teaspoon almond extract	*2 eggs*
3 cups cake flour, sifted	*1 egg yolk*
1 Tablespoon whiskey	*36 blanched almonds*

Cream butter and sugar. Add remaining ingredients except egg yolk, whiskey and almonds. Roll dough on floured board and form into 4 rolls 1" in diameter. Cut off 1" pieces and small into small balls. Press down on greased baking sheet. Press an almond into each cookie. Combine egg yolk and whiskey and brush over top. Bake at 375 for 8 to 12 minutes. Cool on rack.

"The woman was poisoned and the poison was added to her soup. None of the others who tasted the soup have suffered any adverse reaction."

"Not yet. And, how do we know how many people tasted the soup? Only an extremely crude, ill mannered individual would taste their soup before the toasts were completed and the hostess raised her spoon giving the signal to begin. I doubt seriously if any of our other guests would have been so gauche." She hesitated and turned to the widower. "Oh, I'm sorry."

"That's quite all right. She never could resist a good gazpacho. And, she's extremely subtle. Or was. No one even noticed that she pre-tasted."

"I pre-tasted." Dr. Franklin was contrite.

"You did?"

"And, I'm fine. And the gazpacho was excellent. It was not the soup. Something was added to Mrs. Trumpet's soup."

"I pre-tasted". Everett had returned from his brief sojourn with the others in the living room. "I pre-tasted and I'm fine too. It wasn't the soup."

"You see, it was murder!!" Jack Trumpet slumped into his chair and dropped his plugged head into his tiny hands. "Why oh why oh why" he sobbed. "She didn't have an enemy in the world. Why?"

"Marla, sit down. Please." Elmore Franklin had known Marla forever. The kindly family doctor had been the one who'd given her the sedative after she'd been given the news that they'd found Ledge's body. He had signed Waldo Saltonstall's death certificate after he shot himself and he had been the one to diagnose Lorraine Saltonstall's Alzheimer's. Elmore Franklin, with his cheery pink face and off color jokes was Marla's angel of death. Elmore Franklin stood over Marla holding the half-empty paper packet of Mr. Woo's herbs. "Marla, I don't know quite how to say this, so I'll just say it. What is this? What's in this package? Or should I say what *was* in this package?"

"That's nothing. It's just something for my nerves. It's nothing." Marla could feel her innards squirm.

"Marla, dear, please understand that I have to ask you this. You were seen surreptitiously sprinkling something into Mrs. Trumpet's soup plate. I hate to ask you this, but would you care to explain?"

Old Mr. Young was by her side. "You don't have to answer, dear."

"I didn't do anything. I have nothing to hide. I only sprinkled those herbs into the teacup of hot water Acumulada brought me. It was next to Barbie Lee's soup plate, but it was in my teacup. It was not her soup. I didn't touch her soup. I put it in my teacup."

"Teacup? I didn't have a teacup at my place. Did anyone else have a teacup?" Dr. Franklin was gentle yet probing.

"Acumulada brought me hot water to make my herbal tea. Isn't that right, Acumulada? Please tell them. Tell them it was herbs for my tea."

Dr. Elmore Franklin was reaching for the paper packet that sat half empty now at Marla's place.

"She knew I needed it so she brought the hot water to me."

"Did you ask her for it?"

"I never need to ask Acumulada for anything. She always just knows what I need when I need it. I don't know how."

The imposing men turned to the tiny dark woman, the tiny dark woman with the sparkling dental work. "Can you confirm this?"

"Si."

CHAPTER 18

▼

Marla was dumbfounded. People didn't go around murdering people. And, especially, in the middle of what was going to be a lovely meal. Ledge, of course, he had been murdered, but that was quite different. Marla was sure Florence Bainbridge's son (or maybe Florence herself) had him shot and stuffed into the trunk of the car. That was a professional job and done very neatly. The Bainbridges at least had the good sense to hire someone who knew what they were doing and certainly didn't spoil someone's dinner party. But this. This was unacceptable. Here she was, in her own dining room, here was her lifelong friend, this kindly, gentle man, her family doctor, her former primary health care provider accusing her. Standing over her and accusing her. Not exactly accusing her, but questioning, wondering. It wouldn't take much to go from his gentle nudging questions to full fledged accusations. Elmore Franklin wanted to know what was in Mr. Woo's packet. He clearly suspected that she'd slipped Barbie Lee a mickey.

Marla needed an ally, someone who could vouch for her, who could explain what it was she was doing with that incriminating packet of unidentifiable herbs. She looked imploringly at Acumulada.

"Missus Marla uses those leaves from the Chinaman for her headaches. She gets bad headaches. I don't think those leaves help. I could give her better leaves. In my country we have better cures for the headache, than those, but she likes those from the Chinaman."

Marla picked up the Wedgewood teacup into which she'd sprinkled the concoction. A tiny amount remained in the bottom. She raised the cup to her lips. Fuller Arden, Detective Fuller Arden of the Hammerston Auxiliary Police Department intercepted her hand mid lift. "I'm sorry, Mrs. Stone. I'm afraid I'm going to have to ask you not to drink that. I'll be needing that to bring down to the police lab for a forensic analysis."

"Fuller", she beseeched the young man she'd known since childhood. "You can't possibly think ..."

"Mrs. Stone, as of this moment, I'm no longer your sons' childhood friend, I'm an officer of the law. I need to follow procedure. I'll be taking that teacup and its contents in for evidence."

Old Mr. Young was at Marla's side. "Now see here, Fuller. You can't treat this woman that way. She's a respected member of the community. Hell, she's the most respected member this community and this club has. My God, man, she's Marla Stone. What in tarnation are you thinking?"

"Mr. Young, there are procedures to follow and I'll be following them."

"Fuller, you're not even a real police officer." Old Mr. Young had a point. After he had washed out of astronaut training, Fuller had volunteered as an auxiliary police officer in Hammerston, a job which didn't require too much of a time commitment. Mostly, he raised money for the force by selling tickets to his friends for the Police Benevolent Society and playing in the annual softball game against the fire department. He did, though, watch enough television to know the routine.

"I'm afraid that with the way the weather is tonight, I'm going to be the best you can get. Until the storm lets up and we can get some detectives out here, I'm the man on the scene. This is my case. And, Mrs. Stone, I'm afraid, this is my collar. I'm going to have to place you under arrest. You have the right to remain silent ..."

Patrick raced breathlessly into the room. "The bridge is out, the roads are closed, the phone lines are down."

The full moon and high tide during the height of the storm had combined with the high winds to effectively sever Marla's little island from the rest of the world. There was no outside contact. No way to get in or out. Ever the wordsmith, Patrick moaned, "We're in deep doo doo."

"We need a cell phone. Who's got one?" Fuller was relishing his new role. He was taking charge. Not only had he actually tackled and dropped a real live black guy, a football player. He was conducting a real live homicide investigation.

"I've already checked," Patrick replied.

No one dared bring a cell phone into one of Marla's parties.

"You know how she feels about them."

Marla, now under virtual house arrest remained seated at her head of the table. Under arrest or not, she still maintained her decorum and, she still maintained her insistence that a cell phone was absolutely verboten while she was entertaining.

"There is positively no reason why anyone would have to make or receive a phone call during a dinner party. What is there that needs to be said on a phone during a dinner party. 'I'm here. We're having gazpacho. Where are you? Can you hear me?' I still refuse to see why anyone would need to bring one."

Old Mr. Young, never the first in his crowd to have the latest electronic gadget answered her. "You know dear, these are extenuating circumstances. At a time like this, a cell phone would come in rather handy. We've got a dead woman here. We need some professional intervention." He paused and then, suddenly, was inspired. "What about the cars? All of you people must have phones in the car".

"Of course we do, that's it!!" Fuller was elated. Already he had solved the case.

"I've already checked", Patrick said. "All the cars are in the garage. There's no way anyone can get to them until the power comes back on and we can open the garage doors."

Before Lorenzo had gone home for the night, he had taken each guest's car and locked it away in what was now the impenetrable fortress of Ledge's crazy car vault.

"We'll just have to wait, bide our time, twiddle our thumbs. This storm can't last forever."

Fuller swaggered over to Patrick. "And, once it does, we'll be able to take our perp down to headquarters for questioning."

"Perp?"

"Perp. I'm afraid our hostess was seen sprinkling something into Mrs. Trumpet's soup." He turned to Marla. "Isn't that correct, Mrs. Stone? The victim expired from cyanide poisoning. One plus one makes two."

"Marla!" Patrick was horrified. "How could you?" He was suddenly conspiratorial. "Don't worry, hon, I won't mention what you said about you-know-who and the 13 week thing."

"You-know-who, what?" Fuller was not going to let a clue slip through his fingers.

"Patrick, I didn't say anything about you-know-who", Marla insisted. "And, besides, I didn't mean it."

"What exactly did she say?" Fuller asked.

"You don't have to answer, dear," Old Mr. Young reassured her.

"I won't tell them, don't worry. My lips are sealed." Patrick locked his lips shut with an invisible key that he then threw over his shoulder. "You can count on me."

After about four seconds of silence, Patrick was close to bursting; he could stand it no longer. "It was just that she was upset when she realized that the only way she could host the show on her own and get rid of Mrs. Trumpet as her co-host was if Mrs. Trumpet made the decision herself or", he paused for dramatic effect. "If Mrs. Trumpet was no longer around."

"Is this true, Marla?" Old Mr. Young asked.

"No, it's not true." Marla was indignant. "Well, yes it's true that that's how the contract is worded, but it's not like that. I would never do anything to …" The onset of the rare tear began to well up in the corner of her right eye. "Mr. Young, you know I would never, could never … Oh, God. How long have you known me? You know I couldn't do anything like this." Marla let her head drop into her hands. The coolness of her hands felt surprisingly pleasant on her scalp. The herbs had worked. The migraine had been staved off. Thank you, Dr. Woo.

The flickering candles on the table suddenly caught a glimmer of gold tooth and Acumulada was center stage holding a cup of steaming water. "Dar me lo. Dar me lo". She tore the Wedgewood teacup, the evidence from Fuller's hand and, in one fluid motion dumped the steaming water into the cup, swirled the settled residue and raised it to her lips. She threw back the bubbling potion. "It's herbs, herbs from the Chinaman for Mrs. Marla's headaches. Nothing here would do anything to that one. This is just for Mrs. Marla's headaches." She stood, proud, confident and alive. "See, I drink it - nothing. This is just for Mrs. Marla's headaches."

CHAPTER 19

▼

Fuller was crestfallen. His prime suspect had slipped through his fingers. There was nothing in the packet except herbs Marla used as a headache remedy. That crazy housekeeper of hers had proven that. But, if not Marla, then who? He drew back the heavy crewel embroidered drapes covering the library windows and watched the rain relentlessly beat against the glass. How long before it stopped? How much time did he have to find the murderer, solve the case and prove himself before the regular officers of the Hammerston Police Department arrived and relied on him to do what he was really good at – selling tickets to the Policeman's Ball, playing in the softball game and getting their coffee.

So far, Fuller's life had been one disappointment after another. He'd been decidedly average at Choate and at Dartmouth, had excelled only in skiing and kayaking. His attempt to make a living as a mountain guide in Montana had met the same fate as his start up company marketing scuba trips to dive Cane Bay in St. Croix. His failure to make the cut in astronaut training was almost as low to his ego as flunking out of flight attendant training had been. If this law enforcement thing didn't work out, all that was left to Fuller Arden III was a vice presidency in the investment banking firm of Yves, Arden & Brooks. Sure, the starting salary plus bonuses of half a million would be fine, but it wouldn't change his lifestyle. Fuller Arden III had been collecting his generous monthly allowance from Old Mr. Young since college. His father had seen to that. No, money was not an issue for Fuller. But, there was something lacking in his life. He wanted to be a success in something that wasn't handed to him, something that he had done on his own, something that his father had nothing to do with. That something was law enforcement and this murder which had fallen right into his lap, was his ticket to greatness. This was his big break. This is where he could make his name. He could prove to the regular cops that he was good for more than just beating the fire department at shortstop. With his lousy luck, though, the rain would stop, the electricity would come back on, someone would retrieve their cell phone and call the HPD and the "professionals" would step in and Fuller would be relegated to his accustomed minor supporting role.

Pretty face, straight white teeth, strong back. If anyone needed a skier or kayaker, Fuller was the go-to man. Wait. No. No. What if someone asked him to take a kayak across to go into town to get the police? What if that ended up being his only role in this, the crime of the century? What if his golden opportunity turned into just one more stupid frat house keg jump? He did have that old rotator cuff injury, the one he'd gotten in that stupid frat house keg jump. If that decided to suddenly act up, no one could ask him to kayak across or swim across or rebuild the goddamn bridge across. All that he would have would be his mind. All that he could rely on would be his mind. Yes, that was it. He could pretend that he was only relying on his mind.

"A penny for your thoughts, Fuller." Lucretia Franklin's sequins reflected in the windowpane. He turned.

"Oh, Mrs. Franklin, I didn't hear you come in."

"This is just awful. Who would ever have imagined. And, Marla Stone of all people. Who would ever have suspected?"

"Mrs. Stone didn't do it." Arden was, at the same time, disappointed and relieved that his longtime friend had had nothing to do with the murder.

"But, the drugs. People saw her put those drugs into the gazpacho. It was a perfectly brilliant ploy. Who would have noticed with all that, green stuff floating all over that soup?"

"Gazpacho. And, it wasn't drugs, Mrs. Franklin. Mrs. Stone was making tea for herself. She was sprinkling herbs into a cup of hot water that Acumulada had brought her. They're just herbs from Mr. Woo."

"The herbalist?"

"The herbalist."

"Why, I had no idea." She paused. "My God. If I had known she had those drugs, if I had known that crazy Chinaman she sees had those drugs, I could have …" Her voice trailed off and she refocused on the subject at hand.

"What about you Fuller? You look like you could use some herbs? What's wrong with your arm?"

Fuller tired to replicate a look he'd once seen in some movie. Was it Rocky II or III? He wanted to assume Sylvester Stallone's expression as he shrugged off the intense pain his torn rotator cuff was radiating through every nerve of his body. Fuller actually didn't remember any intense pain this injury had every caused him, drunk as he was during the initial keg jump which caused it and dutifully taking his Percoset every four hours after the surgery. But, surely, a torn rotator cuff must cause intense pain. "Oh, it's nothing." He winced and hugged himself. "It's just this old rotator cuff thing. It's never been right since the surgery. And, with this rain and all."

"Was that what you hurt at that frat party thing? Your mother told me about that."

"It was a real injury, Mrs. Franklin." Fuller was having a little difficulty assessing Lucretia's faith in the severity of his injury.

"I'll get my husband. Maybe he has something in his bag. He often does. Besides, it'll give him a chance to tell you again about the time he missed that plane. I swear, if I hear that dodging-the-bullet story one more time, it will be the last." She gripped the wings of the leather chair in front of the window.

"I've already heard that story, Mrs. Franklin. About spending an extra day in Cincinnati to check out that hair removal laser that Conglomotron makes? Why, geez, Mrs. Franklin, if it hadn't been for that Conglomotron laser, you'd be a widow now, wouldn't you?"

"Yes, Fuller. Yes, I would. I'd be a very rich widow. But, no. Thanks to the Conglomotron hair removal laser, my lovely husband is still with us. Yes, Fuller, without Coglomotron, without Jack Trumpet, I'd be a widow. Why am I not smiling?" She released her death grip on the Moroccan leather. "I'll go get him. He'll give you something for that shoulder." She looked over the tops of her half glasses directly into Fuller's soul. "Is it your right shoulder or left?"

Addie Coolidge stood silently over an inconsolable Jack Trumpet who was stretched out on the chaise in the solarium. Her feathers cast eerie shadows in the candlelight.

"What will I do without her, my little dumpling, my little bootsie, my little sugarplum." Few of these sobriquets seemed appropriate for the recently departed Mrs. Trumpet, yet he continued. "My honey lamb," he moaned. "My snuggle bunny. It must have been so awful for her to have tasted that dreadful stuff. She could never stand almonds … and now." He rolled his eyes heavenward, "Now this is the taste she will carry with her for all eternity. There is just no justice. Just no justice."

He brightened momentarily when Acumulada walked in. "Bring me a bone dry Gray Goose martini, would you sweetheart? A double. Thanks a lot."

"Do you think fire water is the answer?" Addie's recently acquired Native American persona overlapped a tiny bit with her last reinvention of herself, that of her tea totaling Quaker forebears. Unlike the Pochahontas connection, the Quakers were at least biologically related to Addie, not just in-laws.

"Trying to numb your feelings with fire water is never the answer. We should join hands and pray together to the Great Spirit. We can get through this together. The killer will be brought to justice. I'm sure our Fuller will see to it. He's a bright boy and comes from a wonderful family."

"It was him you know. I'm sure of it."

"Fuller?" Addie gasped.

"Not Fuller. That wife murderer, P.D. Quinn. He did it. Who let that man into this house? He has a record of violence. He did it. I'm sure of it. Those coloreds. Can't trust them for a minute. And a jock to boot."

Addie was indignant. "Are you insinuating that since Mr. Quinn is a minority he's immediately a suspect? Since he's a member of a population that's been oppressed and downtrodden, he would naturally resort to violence? That rather than deal with a dispute on a rational basis, violence would be his first choice? Is that what you're suggesting?"

"Minority," Trumpet snorted. "He's no more a minority than I am. Have you ever seen where he lives? What he drives? Where he plays golf? We should all be so downtrodden."

"Mr. Trumpet, my people have been discriminated against for centuries." Addie adjusted her buckskin dress. "When the white man came and took our lands, it changed forever the course of our history."

"Oh, for chrissakes." He brightened momentarily when he noticed Acumulada's golden tooth flickering in the candlelit doorway. She was deep in thought, holding his Grey Goose.

"I hope that's for me, toots."

"Mister, may I say to you? If it's all right? May I say?"

"What are you talking about?" His gratitude at the prompt delivery of his Grey Goose only went so far.

"The black man with the big bottom, he's not who did it. Why would he hurt Mrs. Barbie Lee? If that big black man wanted to hurt someone, it would be you, Mister Jack Trumpet."

"Me?"

"Aren't you the one who cancelled his contract, Mister?"

Addie's bleeding heart began again in earnest. "Is this true, Mr. Trumpet? Did you cancel the contract of an African American? Did you deprive an African American male the opportunity to earn a living for himself and his family?"

His eyes narrowed. "For a housekeeper, she's pretty up to date on her gossip."

"Si, Mister."

Trumpet took the high road. "So what if I did. I can't have a wife murderer stay on as spokesman of one of Conglomotron's companies. Here we are trying to sell garden equipment and sporting goods and this crazy bastard, our spokesman, bludgeons his wife with the Congo Driver – our goddamn golf club, the club he's supposed to be representing. Not a smart plan. Not a smart plan at all."

Addie was intrigued. "Why on earth would he want to kill your wife? That makes no sense. Acumulada is absolutely right. If P.D. Quinn were going to kill anyone, surely it would be you."

For once, Jack Trumpet was silent. His face reflected the serene understanding of a man who had at last learned the eternal truth.

"That's it!! He was after me, all along and my poor little flufferbunny had the incredibly bad luck of taking a bullet for me."

"A bullet?" Addie was confused. "I thought you said she was poisoned."

"She was poisoned. That was just a figure of speech, honey. But, she sat in my seat. The seat that was meant for me. Don't you get it? We changed seats. She can't handle light coming at her from her right, so I changed seats with her so the candles would shine on the side of her face where the implants had already healed. She was taking antibiotics. We think she may have had a little cellulitis from those implants." He lowered his voice almost to a whisper. "The right side was never right. She knew it, too, poor little love." He sighed. "All the pain she went through with those implants. They were going to make the difference for her, you know, with her television career. That old Gifford broad, she had a crooked nose and boobs the size of a sow's udder, but she had cheekbones, and those made all the difference." His face took on a pensive wandering look. "If only … she was this close to stardom … if only."

"If only what, Mr. Trumpet." Fuller had somehow acquired a clipboard and was taking extensive notes as he interrogated each of the dinner guests. It was now Jack Trumpet's turn to answer Fuller's questions.

"Do I assume, Mr. Arden, that you are here in some official capacity. Are you an officer of the law, Mr. Arden?"

"I am sir. I am a special auxiliary patrolman with the Hammerston Police Department, sworn to uphold the law of this town and of this county."

Fuller seemed to have grown. He was taller, he was self assured, he was in charge. Just to be on the safe side, though, he alternated holding first his left arm then his right, close to his body as if it were in an invisible sling. He was having just one heck of a time trying to remember which rotator cuff it was that he'd hurt. Seeing his stoic uncomplaining acceptance of his incredible pain, no one would dare suggest that he swim or kayak across into town to fetch the police. For the moment, he *was* the police.

CHAPTER 20

▼

Florence Bainbridge was not a patient woman. She had things to do; things which certainly did not include sitting around in Marla's living room while this little Hardy Boy interrogated every guest. She and Everett were leaving for South America in three days and she had barely begun packing. She never could remember. If it was spring in the Northern Hemisphere, was it summer, winter or fall in the Southern? Should she pack fur or was it enough to bring a cashmere in every color. She made a mental note to have Everett call the travel agent in the morning. The morning. It practically *was* morning and here they all were. Waiting for the rain to stop; waiting for the power to come back on; waiting for the garage doors to be opened and the cars to be retrieved; waiting, waiting, waiting. She had no time. She had no time.

Marla and Acumulada exploded into the room. "We've made contact with the outside world. Sort of". Marla was euphoric.

"Si. We can hear them. They don't hear us".

Fuller examined the boom box Acumulada carried. It looked like a small radio/tape player, but it was crank operated. Through its translucent case its clockwork innards were visible.

"No batteries?"

"No batteries. All you do is crank it up and it lasts for quite a long time, don't you think so, Acumulada?"

"A little while I think. Not so long. Batteries they would be better. Why didn't you get some missus?"

Marla, the ever ready, had delegated that particular task. At least she thought she'd delegated that task. Her housekeeper had forgotten to keep the closet stocked. She was sure she had reminded her. She was positive. She'd used the entire supply he had in the house for her home repair class the day they were working on an emergency survival kit. She assumed an air of the aggrieved victim, yet she was never before so irritated that she hadn't included preparing one for herself.

The skinny Latina did not buy her act.

"Missus, I told you. When you went to the big dirty store. I told you."

"It doesn't matter who reminded who now, does it. We have no batteries and there's nothing we can do about it."

"Whom," Acumulada quietly corrected.

"What?"

"Whom. It doesn't matter who reminded whom. 'Whom' is the object of the sentence. My English teacher ..."

Marla could take no more. "Oh, bugger off, for god's sake. Who, whom, what bloody difference does it make?"

Acumulada recoiled momentarily, but stood her ground. "It should be whom, that's all. Native speakers should set a good example for us."

"She's quite right. We native speakers should set a good example for the servant class. It should be 'whom'". Walter Coolidge was always ready to throw his Brahmin weight around and lobby for the courtly treatment of his inferiors. The fact that his lobbying did not include trivial matters like equal pay, better benefits or job security was never bothersome to him.

He turned his skunk like face toward Acumulada. "That's very good, my dear." He raised his gnarled, arthritic hand and patted her head. "You should be proud of yourself for noticing that bit of grammatical inaccuracy, Immaculada."

"Merci, senor, but it's Acumulada."

"Yes, whatever." Walter resumed his reading by candlelight. *Barrons* had been his weekly bible for 46 years and this little nonsense was not going to deprive him of keeping up with Wall Street.

"Fuller, let me take a look at that thing." Everett Bainbridge strode over to Fuller to examine this curious battery free contraption. Everett, long the luggage carrier for his well preserved and well traveled wife felt it was time to assert himself. He'd not always been a CEO, negotiating acquisitions, LBO's and labor contracts. Although he'd never really used it, his bachelor's degree was in mechanical engineering. Once his little medical instruments company went public and was then acquired by Conglomotron, he'd "retired". Although he was then only 35, he took advantage of an opportunity that would probably never again present itself. Florence had all but insisted. She'd had plans. She had no intention of spending the best years of her life entertaining the deadeningly boring wives of vice presidents and sales managers while her husband climbed the corporate ladder. As long as he had the chance to leap frog to the top and then jump off, he'd damn well better take it or he'd find himself doing that corporate ladder thing as a solo act. He'd acquiesced and established the predictable pattern for their marriage.

For the first time in as long as he could remember, his mechanical engineering background leant him a certain amount of expert status. He was the one who should check out the operation of a radio. He should take charge. His Rob Roys had worn off sufficiently so that he could actually participate in the evening. "I think I saw one of these things when I was at Dinah Shore's house. I've told you about that evening, haven't I?"

✳   ✳   ✳   ✳

ROB ROY

2 jiggers dry vermouth	*7 jiggers Scotch*

Stir well with ice cubes. Add 1 dash angostura bitters and a twist of lemon peel.

The level of interest in Everett's "relationship" with Dinah Shore could be summed up in a word: none.

"We'd played golf one afternoon and then she invited a couple of us back to her house for drinks." He gazed into the middle distance, lovingly recalling his afternoon with Dinah Shore. His and the dozens of others who'd anted up the $5,000.00 to play in her charity golf tournament. "What a talent." The middle distance was once again his universe. "She walked over to the piano and sang, just like that. Ah, what a talent."

Florence Bainbridge's recently lifted eyes shot her husband one of her "looks". "Did Dinah Shore have one of these radios, darling? Do you know how it works?"

"Yes, sweetheart, I believe she did." He furrowed his brow and shut his eyes tightly, index fingers, left and right, keeping time with the thoughts in his head. "Or was it Ethel Kennedy? Could have been Ethel, now that I think of it. Not really sure. Ethel or Dinah Shore."

"It really doesn't matter, does it, darling? Ethel Kennedy, Dinah Shore, it really doesn't matter. It's the radio that's important. Do you know how these things work?" Right about now, Florence Bainbridge, would have been happy to have given every bit of gold jewelry she owned to get out of this house and home. She needed to be home. She needed to listen to this radio, figure out what was going on in the world and get *home*. This was not just a little storm, a power outage. This was a terrorist attack. This was something big and she needed to be in her own house with her own clothes and her own shoes. She needed to get out of here.

"It's nothing more than a wind up mechanism like a clock's works," Everett said. "This handle here."

Fuller forgot and foolishly used what should have been his useless right hand to wind the handle ten, twenty, thirty solid rotations.

"That arm feeling better, Fuller?" Elmore Franklin M.D., the master diagnostician rarely missed a thing. At the moment the question left Dr. Franklin's lips, Fuller remembered to wince. Unfortunately, the wince was like what you'd find in a badly dubbed Japanese movie – just the tiniest bit off. "Not really, Dr. Franklin. I just think it's better to try to work through it - play with the pain. You know how it is, don't you?" He grinned his best boyish grin, "Coach?"

"Not really. But, it doesn't matter. Let's take a look at that radio."

Fuller was madly spinning the dial, with his less than dexterous left hand. The box was his clumsy dance partner as he dipped it this way, turned it that way, searching for something other than static. Finally, success.

The disembodied voice called everyone to its presence. The odd little group gathered round and worshiped at its clear plastic altar, the duplicate of which resided in the home of Dinah Shore, or was it Ethel Kennedy. They stared at it, waiting for what? A picture? A revelation? Instead of a picture what they got was the relieved voice of Charles Goodnough, longtime WGBH announcer. Ordinarily, he would have been here at The Club meeting, but had committed himself to working an extra shift at the station. He was doing that a lot lately. The show he'd pitched to the 'GBH brass had managed to get him demoted from "senior news analyst" Monday through Friday to utility weekends cover-the-snowstorm-on-location-extra-shift guy almost overnight. No one was more surprised than Charles that the radio station balked at the idea of a mime show. What was better than mime? These people were brilliant. A radio mime show could work. They could be the first station in the country to do it. It had never been done. All it would take was the rich resonant voice of Charles Goodnough describing the action. Who wouldn't love that? Who wouldn't love living in a city whose public radio station had the prescience to bring mime to the airways. Who wouldn't love being the first in the whole country? The executives at 'GBH had no foresight. They had no courage. So, Charles Goodnough had been demoted to weekends and snowstorms. He had no choice; he needed the health insurance.

Patrick strode over and patted the radio, congratulating the mechanical device for doing what it was designed to do. "You know, Fuller, what GBH stands for, don't you?"

Fuller groaned. Marla made a mental note to remember this very moment the next time she was tempted to even consider Patrick as a life partner.

"What an extraordinary job Bos-Ed has done throughout this whole crisis. It's quite remarkable really, that within such a short period of time, all of their customers have had their power restored. What team work, what advance planning, what a remarkable system."

"What a load of shit" Patrick was on his feet. "Our power has not been *restored.* What the hell are we? Chopped liver? Don't we count? Are we not part of their *system?* Their *network?* Their *grid?* When is our power going to be restored? When? When? When? We have a situation here. We have a serious situation on our hands here that needs to be addressed."

Charles Goodnough's sonorous voice continued. "Even though the rain continues in some areas, we are assured by Bos-Ed that the crisis is totally under control and none of their customers are without power."

Acumulada's brows furrowed as she thought about the correction. "Shouldn't that be 'is'?"

"Oh, for Gods's sake, go look it up." Even Patrick's patience was wearing thin. He turned to the woman he thought he knew. "Marla", Patrick's tone was accusatory. "Marla, you are a Bos-Ed customer, aren't you?"

"Of course. There must be some mistake. Of course I'm a Bos-Ed customer. Hammerston is in the BosEd area and we're part of Hammerston. It's just that …" Her voice trailed off.

"Just that what?"

Marla walked across the palace sized Kerman rug and perched on the arm of the leather sofa across which Lulu had sprawled her fluffy body.

"I'm really a little embarrassed, but I feel I must admit it." Every eye in the room fixed on her. Elmore and Lucretia Franklin, the Bainbridges, Walter and Addie, Patrick and Pam and Fuller and even Jack Trumpet stared at Marla who was staring imploringly, holding both hands of Lulu Noone.

"Lulu, do you remember when Ledge was buying up all of your paintings? The ones with the neon? The ones that had to be installed? Do you remember that, Lulu?"

Lulu Noone's cropped salt and pepper head bobbed up and down. "Of course I remember that. That man was a saint. He was solely responsible for my success as an artist. For my acceptance into the world of serious art." The bobbing of her bristly head only served to increase the blood flow to her already florid face.

"Well," Marla hesitated. "I'm not at all proud of this … I don't really know how to say it, so I guess I'll just say it."

She inhaled deeply and rose, standing at attention facing with dignity the firing squad assembled in her library.

"There was a man, a man I didn't know very well, a man I met, a man Ledge introduced me to actually, a man who called himself Neon Jimmy."

Lulu was jet propelled off the couch. "Neon Jimmy!! He installed all of my best paintings. He's my installer!! He's my neon supplier."

She paused, her face darkening in remembering. "At least he used to be my neon supplier. He claims they can't get that neon anymore. He claims it's been," she curled the first two fingers of both hands into quotation marks in the air "discontinued". She narrowed her eyes to slits and glared at Jack trumpet. "But, we know better, don't we, Mr. Trumpet?"

"Could we please stay on task. Focus. Stay on target. Stick to the topic."

Patrick's usual mild demeanor had begun to seriously recede, revealing an impatience Marla had never seen before. Yet another confirmation of her growing realization that Patrick the blind man was destined for a life with someone other than Marla Stone. He turned his impatient face toward Marla. "You and this Neon Jimmy character, you didn't … didn't … you know."

"Oh, for God's sake, of course, not. It's just that I, well, I, er, that is, I …"

"Just spit it out Marla. What are you trying to say?"

Marla took a deep breath and clasped her fine boned hands under chin as if in prayer. On the exhale, barely a whisper: "He connectedmyelectricity."

"What did you say?" Patrick was mystified.

"I'm not proud of it, Patrick. Don't make me repeat it."

"No, really. I couldn't understand one word you said. What you just said sounded like some kind of airport announcement. What did you say?"

She could postpone no longer. "He connected my electricity to something. I don't know exactly what. Some kind of line out here on the island. I don't know what. But, ever since he did it, I haven't gotten a bill. I don't think BosEd knows I'm here."

"Marla."

"Mrs. Stone".

"Marla. I'm shocked."

"Who is this guy? What did he connect to?" Jack Trumpet could barely contain his interest. If anyone was going to score free electricity, Jack Trumpet needed to be in on the deal.

"Missus, you didn't have to tell them. Nobody needed to know this. It could have just been you and me."

"I. You and I."

"Si. You and I. Sorry.

Having bared her soul, Marla felt relieved. She'd been a young single mother when it happened. She'd been desperate. Maybe it was a mistake, but once she'd agreed to it, there had been no turning back. Now, it was all out in the open. If she were scorned by her friends and neighbors, so be it. She had confessed. Now that she had this deal to do those television shows for Jack trumpet's cable station, now that she could expect to have a little more income than the pittance that her classes brought in, she'd be able to pay back all the charges. She would throw herself on the mercy of the electric company. She would pay them everything she owed plus interest. They would have to accept. Wouldn't they? They couldn't refuse to supply someone with electricity. Wasn't electricity a constitutional right? She was sure they'd forgive her now that she'd confessed.

The dinner guests all betrayed emotions ranging from puzzlement to shock to horror to pity.

"It's all right, dear. No one blames you." Lucretia Franklin's kindness was almost more than Marla could bear.

"People should blame me. I stole from the electric company." Tears were starting to well up.

"It's just, dear, that we're concerned that we're going to be stranded here for who knows how long. It's not as if we dislike your house. It's charming, certainly. You always do things so beautifully. But, we need to know when we're going to be able to leave. Dr. Franklin has patients and I have a bromeliad meeting."

Despite the fact that she'd been denied her young rich widowhood, Lucretia's bitterness usually extended only to her husband. Towards others, she was the soul of generosity, the sincere soul of generosity. And, it was not just the botanical gardens which was a recipient of her largesse. The library, the community theatre, the historical society, the symphony, the museum, all owed a debt to Lucretia Franklin. What Addie Coolidge and Florence Bainbridge did with a checkbook (tax deductible) Lucretia did with her time, her presence and her connections.

"You won't be stranded here forever, Lucretia, don't worry. I've got a group coming in who's going to use the house next week. The group is arriving Monday. It's a matrix regression therapy group. The facilitator will be here tomorrow afternoon to set up."

Addie, who'd been on the verge of dozing for quite a while, suddenly lit up as if she'd just seen Elvis. "Bomatumbi Mabatata?"

"Yes. He's doing a workshop on healing past life memories."

"Oh, Marla, you simply must let me stay. I did one of his workshops several years ago. You must let me stay. That was when I connected so strongly to my Native American roots. I journeyed to the bardos and freed myself of unwanted spirit attachments, creating the space for my new found Native American spirits to inhabit my soul. It was quite thrilling. Do you know I was able to remember the death transition? You've simply got to let me stay."

"I don't know, Addie. His group is already made up. I think there are six or seven. They probably won't be able to fit any more in. You know how those matrix regression therapy groups are structured."

"The good news, though, is that we'll be out of here by tomorrow afternoon at the latest, is that what you're saying, Marla?" Florence Bainbridge was beginning to soften. Being trapped with a definite release date was not half as bad as that indefinite sentence. With any luck, this could turn into a little adventure.

"Maybe we should all just go upstairs and get some sleep until those people come tomorrow to re-script their karmic conflicts." She flashed a smile at her fellow Club members. "I'll bet Marla has every one of those bedrooms upstairs made up just waiting for all those matrix regression people to sleep in. Betcha." She winked at Marla. "Am I right? We can use them."

"No one is going anywhere." Fuller needed to exert some control over this group. "Are you all forgetting that we have," he grimaced in the general direction of Jack Trumpet. "A dead body in the diningroom? There are things that must be attended to."

"Damn right they must be attended to. For once, this little guy and I here agree on something. Now, Officer Fulton, arrest this woman. This electricity stealing criminal. Anybody who'd steal electricity from a public utility, a company licensed and authorized by the Commonwealth of Massachusetts to provide electric service to the population. Jesus H. Christ." Jack Trumpet roared. He was elated. "You're the criminal. I'll be goddamned. You of all people!! You're the criminal. Hey kid," he called to Fuller, "Get over here and do your duty. Arrest this woman."

"I don't think this is exactly criminal, Mr. Trumpet. It's probably more of a civil matter." He straightened his spine, "And, it's Fuller."

"Whatever. Listen, we're going to be stuck here with this criminal woman in the dark in her house until when? Monday? Tuesday? Wednesday? Until somebody happens to drive along and see the bridge out and take a boat across to find us? Is that it? We're supposed to just sit here? Send smoke signals? Hoping to be found? I don't think so. Listen, my wife is in that dining room dead as a haddock and the man," he glared accusingly at Marla, "or is it 'the woman' who poisoned her is sitting right here in this room. I suggest, Mr. Fulton or Fuller Howdy Doody that you do something abut this pdq. I'm talking now, Mister."

I'm doing the best I can, Mr. Trumpet. Have you been paying attention? There's a large group coming in on Monday and the facilitator will be here tomorrow afternoon. He'll see that the bridge is out and get help. We'll just have to wait until then."

"I don't want to wait. I haven't got time to wait. You claim to be some kind of law enforcement officer. Enforce, pal. I'm talking now. We haven't got time to wait."

Pam suddenly found her voice. She rose to her full five feet one half inch. The kelly green Jacqlyn Smith she'd purchased especially for tonight could barely contain her pent up rage.

She whispered and every eye turned in her direction. "Don't speak to him that way. Don't you dare speak to him that way. You, you, you …"

The hand of God turned up the volume on Pam's voice. No longer mealy mouthed, she bellowed, "You snake; you liar; you emu fraud; you daddy napper."

"Now, see here, little lady? Who do you think you're talking to? I'll thank you to show a little more respect to your superiors. I'll talk to Mr. Fulton Fuller Fulton any damn way I please. And, to you, I'll thank you to sit down and shut up. I have no idea what you're talking about. Daddy napper? Emu fraud? What is this gibberish?"

"You know very well what I'm talking about. My daddy sank his whole life savings into that emu ranch and your company was supposed to buy him out. That was supposed to be his nest egg – his future, his retirement. But, suddenly, out of the blue, out of no where, no more emus; emus aren't marketable anymore. Conglomotron isn't buying. Your ranch has been removed from the acquisition list. My poor daddy. That's what the letter said. 'Your ranch has been removed from the acquisition list.' He sank everything he had and more into that place. He begged, he borrowed and he stole and then, poof, nothing. He's stuck with all them emus." She gulped, catching her breath. "Well, me and Mama were stuck with them. You ruined his life. He ran off, just disappeared. What could he do? You ruined his life. You ruined Mama's life. You ruined my life. I just hate you. I could just kill you. I could just kill you."

Poor little Pam slumped into Fuller's arms and buried her face in his Harris tweed. On her way into Fuller's jacket, she had yet another humiliation. Glancing down at the carpet around her feet, she noticed the breadcrumbs. At least she thought they were breadcrumbs. They were off white crumbles of something under and emerging from her right shoe and then from her left. Breadcrumbs in Marla Stone's library. Doubtful. Wait. These weren't breadcrumbs. It was the decomposing innersoles of her shoes. The shoes she'd found in the closet. They'd been in there for years, but black pumps are black pumps. She was sure no one would notice that they'd both been gnawed on a little by some sort of rodent which she hoped was only a mouse. She'd worn them and forgotten about them. Until now. The gnawed spot wasn't a "little spot". The entire sole of both shoes had been gnawed through exposing the cork or paper or cardboard that was the lining. The more she moved, the more powder of the cork or paper or cardboard sifted out through the bottoms. She could just cry. She hadn't meant to draw attention to herself, but she just couldn't help it. She was sure everyone had been staring and laughing at her all evening. Then she had to go and have this meltdown to ensure that they would.

"So, the little mouse has roared and could kill me, is that so? Well, well, well, Mr. Fulton Fuller, I'd say we have another suspect sitting here. I'd recommend that you add your little girlfriend here to the group you'll be handing over to the authorities once we made contact with the outside world. It is clear to me that my poor darling wife, my poor Barbie Lee was the innocent victim of someone who was targeting me. Someone who intended to kill me. We did change seats just after everyone sat down, as you well recall. My little lamb sat in the seat that was meant for me. You all here saw that, I'm sure. And, ladies and gentlemen, you also all just heard this young woman clearly and plainly state that she could kill me. Well, I suggest to you that that adds up to a confession. A confession of murder. Wouldn't you agree, Mr. Fulton Fuller?"

Fuller was clearly over his head. "No, certainly not. People don't threaten people after the fact. Besides, pretty much everyone in this room has a motive to kill you, Mr. Trumpet."

"Is that so?"

CHAPTER 21

▼

There was not enough Visene on the planet to allow Marla to actually blink without the clear sensation that a practical joker had replaced her contacts with 0000 sandpaper.

"Missus, did you sleep at all?" The remarkable Acumulada apparently required no sleep whatsoever. There she stood, fully dressed in her pink daytime uniform and black Reeboks, face scrubbed, gold tooth twinkling, black hair pulled severely into the ballerina's chignon at the nape of her neck that she favored, brown eyes brown, whites white.

Marla had never been a slug-a-bed, but Acumulada represented a whole new dimension in energy without the time wasting necessity for sleep. Marla was convinced that she slept for five or six minutes at a clip standing up somewhere in her little pantry downstairs.

"No, Acumulada, I can't say I even closed my eyes once all night. Although we really couldn't call it much of a night, now can we?"

Acumulada, though, apparently did have adequate rest. She deposited the breakfast tray on Marla's bed. A silver pot of coffee, freshly squeezed orange juice, a bowl of Special K and a perfect rose bud.

"I'm sorry I couldn't make the toast, Missus. Still no electric."

Marla winced at the reminder of her humiliation. A shiver ran down her spine.

"Oh, Acumulada, it's perfectly all right. Cold cereal is fine this morning."

Between sips of the revitalizing orange juice, Marla picked up the silver clock on her bedside table and attempted to focus on the hands.

"Two hours, Missus. People went to sleep about three and it's almost five now. That's enough for them, no?" She rolled her remarkably unbloodshot eyes. "Those people! Nobody has nothing. Dio mio. I have to find for everyone toothbrushes, pajamas, a sleep mask for that crazy one. Nobody has nothing. Nada. Lucky for us that foreigner is coming. We could use the things we had ready for his people."

"No one was expecting that they'd have to sleep here last night, dear."

No, no one was expecting they'd have to sleep at Stone's Throw last night. But, sleep there they did. No one was expecting that they'd be trapped here, Shanghaied on this charming private island within sight of the Boston skyline, just as surely as if they'd been somewhere off of Borneo. But, trapped they were. Still, there was no power. Still, no one could get to their cars or to their cell phones to call for help or report that the bridge was out. No one was expecting that there'd be a murder in Marla's dining room, God, just the thought of it – just the word -made Marla shiver, but there it was. A body, big as life, or in this case, death, carefully shrouded in a king size off-white Matelasse coverlet stiffened on her celadon and gold Kerman rug. The heat. The good news was that the house was noticeably chilly. Poor Barbie Lee would keep better.

As she lovingly caressed her steaming coffee cup, warming her hands and transferring that warmth through the rest of her exhausted body, she suddenly shot a question to Acumulada with her eyes.

"I did the coffee the old way. Like we did in my country. With the stove. With the gas."

But, the coffee, the gas. As usual, Acumulada anticipated her next question

"The gas is still on, I guess you pay them, but the heat no good up here. Only downstairs. The machine that pushes the heat up here needs electric. But, downstairs is OK".

"That's not good, Acumulada. We should be warmer and more comfortable up here and downstairs where, the person, the woman, the deceased, the body … Maybe we should move her."

"No problem, Missus. I opened the windows in the diningroom. The stiff is cold."

The stiff. All Marla wanted to do was pull the covers right back over her head and stay there completely covered by her 360 count Egyptian pima cotton sheets until the police could be called and this mess could be taken care of by professionals.

Her only consolation was that this was not a permanent situation. Marla had to continue to reinforce that thought. This was just temporary. Just as soon as

Bomatumbi Mabatata got here later today and began to prepare for his five-day matrix regression therapy workshop, all of this nightmare would be over. Bomatumbi had arranged with Marla to rent Stone's Throw for the next six days. He and his workshop participants would take over the house and grounds for the next week, exploring previous lives, re-scripting unfinished karmic conflicts derived from other lives and remembering the death transition in order to unblock old fears. While he and his group used the house, Marla and Acumulada had plans to reorganize every closet from the root cellar all the way up to the attic furniture storage. She had purchased two new label makers, one for her and one for Acumulada. She was planning to box and then enter everything into a computerized data base. Things were going to get organized. Acumulada had researched the perfect computer software to use for the upcoming household inventory.

Once Bomatumbi drove the three miles in from the road and saw the bridge was gone and all of the power was out, he would notify the authorities and all would be returned to normal. He would most certainly use his cell phone and not rely on spiritual communication with BosEd. He was due at 5:00 p.m. They needed only 12 more hours.

"We should wake them up, Missus."

"Why? Let them sleep. With any luck, they'll all sleep until 5 when Bomatumbi gets here and then just leave, get out of here, go home, go anywhere."

"No, Missus, they have to get up. Arden Fuller needs them to be in the livingroom. He needs to ask them questions. He said."

"His name is Fuller Arden. Fuller is his first name. It's not Arden Fuller."

"No problem."

Marla liked Fuller, despite the fact that he had initially suspected her of Barbie's murder. He was trying to be professional and do what the real police would have done. He was a dear boy, he really was and came from a wonderful family, but she wished he would give up on this idiotic idea of being a junior detective. If he'd just wait until Bomatumbi got here, then the real police could take over. They could do the sorts of things police on television do and get this ridiculous situation behind her. Of course, there was the little matter of her electricity. It would be embarrassing, but she'd simply have to find a way to come up with the cash to pay it off. Patrick. He might be willing. Of course he'd be willing. All she would have to do would be to say "yes". Yes to Patrick. Yes to his marriage proposal and make him the "happiest darn guy on the planet" and spend the rest of her life listening to the derivation of the PBS station's call letters, the same jokes and cute little greetings and adios messages. "Be sure to tell the pilot to have a safe flight. Ha. Ha." Could she do it? Could she stand it? Maybe. But, maybe there was another way. Ledge. Of course. That was it. Ledge. Good old dead Ledge. He'd ordered the illegal electrical hookup. She'd had no idea about it. And, what with his affair with Florence which had sent her into a tailspin, the pending divorce and Ledge's unbelievably complex finances and then his mysterious death which had never been fully explained complicating matters further, how could she have been expected to notice that a BosEd bill hadn't been paid for several years. She could say that someone on her staff actually paid the bills. Yeah, that was it. Acumulada would go along with her, probably, maybe. Please, God, she'd have to. How could someone like Acumulada, an uneducated immigrant, be expected to know how often an electric bill was sent? Acumulada would take the fall for her. Please. She could barely speak English when she set her mind to it. What could she know? Marla could say she had absolutely no idea. She was horrified. Of course, now that she knew, it went without saying that she would repay every penny of the past due bill. Would anyone buy that? It was worth a shot. It was certainly better than stooping to ask Patrick for help.

CHAPTER 22

▼

Everett Bainbridge gazed into the masked face of his wife. The sleep mask that idiotic Hispanic woman had found for her winked back at him. One eye open, one shut, both outlined in multicolored rhinestones. Who in their right mind would actually have bought such an abomination? She snorted her pre-waking snort, eyes fluttering under the mask. It was too early, only a little after five. Florence never awoke this early. That was the whole point of the sleep mask. Ever since the third eye lift, sunlight, gray day light, moonlight, candlelight, light from a refrigerator being opened down the hall, light of any kind awakened the lovely Mrs. Bainbridge before she'd been fully rested and recharged. She couldn't have that. After all the money she'd spent on her eyes, she couldn't risk letting them puff up again from lack of sleep. This morning, though, seemed to be different. This morning, she'd risk it and be up before 11:00 if it meant she could get out of here. She snorted again and pushed the left side, the winking eye side of the mask up to her forehead. Now, she stared back at her husband through one bright, shiny, sequin lined thickly lashed albeit cockeyed eye; the other squinting, watery, red rimmed and begging for mascara.

"I've got to get out of here Ev. You've got to do something."

"What would you suggest I do?"

"You're an engineer. Engineer something."

Every time, every time she wanted something, every time something went wrong, every time the situation seemed impossible, Everett's dear wife decided engineer was a verb.

"You heard Marla. We'll just have to wait. There's nothing I can do until that guy, that witch doctor comes and brings some communication device with him."

"Bomatumbi. Bomatumbi Mabatata."

"Bomatumbi Mabatata my ass. That guy was probably born Earl Leroy Jefferson. Bomatumbi Mabatata." He snorted. "Did the girl bring up any coffee?"

"He's a respected matrix regression therapist. It doesn't matter what his name is in this life. He's had many lives and travels back and forth between them all the time. That's what matrix regression therapy is all about."

"You know him?"

"I know of him." He threw a sideways glance in her direction. "People talk."

"No kidding." Everett was starting to get irritated and his caffeine deprivation was not helping his mood. "She said she'd bring up coffee."

"When did you see her. And, by the way, 'her' name is 'Acumulada'."

"Acumulada. That's another one. What kind of name is that? Why not Bomatumbi II. These people give me the creeps. What is with them?"

"You liked her fine last night when she was bringing you that never ending supply of Rob Roys." Florence adopted a nasal falsetto "Neatly, just how you like them, Mr. Everett."

"I'd like her better if she'd bring up some of that coffee."

"When did she tell you about the coffee?"

"I saw her downstairs earlier. She's able to make coffee" he now tried out the falsetto "like they do in my country." He shrugged. "In her country, they're probably still rubbing sticks together and eating grubs from the undersides of rocks."

Florence pushed the winking side of her sleep mask up and over her brow creating a version of a sequin patterned headband, not unlike the headband Marla had been wearing last evening. She squinted into her diamond Piaget which she'd absolutely refused to remove from her wrist lest the murderer be tempted to add jewel theft to his/her repertoire.

"You must have been up pretty early. It's barely five now."

"You know how I am. Couldn't sleep", said the man who snored loudly through Jay Leno's monologues on a virtually nightly basis. He was particularly hard to stir on those nights when Florence felt amorous. Who would have blamed her for her little tryst with Ledge Stone? Was it her fault that she was an irresistibly attractive sensual being who had the misfortune of being married to an oaf who was more interested in Ethel Kennedy and Dinah Shore and their golf games than he was in his vibrant, youthful looking, very thin wife? Yes, she thought. She knew how he was.

"Were you in the dining room? Did you see the body? Was anyone else there?"

"Just the little spic. Guarding the door like some sphinx at the tomb. Couldn't get near it."

"Why would you want to get near it, dear?"

"Just to see. You know how I am." Hm. Yes. She did. "Guess Walter and Addie felt the same way. Bumped into them on the stairs. They couldn't get their story straight. He said they were looking for water; she said they needed Pepto Bismol. Maybe the water was to wash down the Pepto. Maybe they were on their way back for some other reason."

"Do you think?" Florence was willing to forgive her husband for being the oaf that he was if he had some good dirt to share with her.

"She's just found out about her Indian ancestry, right?"

"She's only an Indian by marriage. Walter's family is descended from Pocahontas. The Boston Coolidges, you know. I'm not sure that makes him an 'Indian'. But, when Addie found out about this Pocahontas lineage, she just ran with it. All of a sudden, she's a downtrodden minority, a member of a poor, mistreated indigenous people. Her people actually were Quakers."

Everett Bainbridge fell into deep thought, evidenced by engaging in what Florence considered one of his more annoying habits. He scratched and scratched the scratched the sandpaper that was his cheeks. Back and forth, back and forth, bristle, bristle, bristle.

"Did you find a razor in Marla's bathroom, dear?" Florence was sometimes just too subtle.

Too engrossed in his scratching to even hear his wife, Everett continued, pondering, staring into space. Suddenly, "It was Conglomotron. It was Trumpet's company. I'm sure of it."

"What was Conglomotron? What are you talking about?"

"When I was with Ethel Kennedy. Down at her place there, Hilshire Farms."

Florence detested his name dropping, but if one were to drop a name, at least it should be correct.

"Hickory Hill"

"Whatever. But, I remember Ethel talking about this Indian reservation, this land right in New Jersey that was essentially being stolen from Pocahontas' tribe and the tribal elders couldn't do a thing about it. It was the most valuable real estate in the state and it turned out it was really owned by this Indian tribe and Jack Trumpet's company snatched it up right out from under them. The Indians didn't get a dime. They got relocated and that was that. Left them pretty pissed off."

Florence was becoming animated, the color was returning to her face. "That's it. Let's go tell Fuller and we can get out of here."

"Tell Fuller what?"

"It was clearly Addie and Walter who killed that little fool, slipping a mickey or some weird Indian brew into what they thought was Jack Trumpet's soup. She ate it. End of story. Fuller will see that instantly. Let's tell and we can finally go home." She implored her husband "Please".

Acumulada had slipped silently into the room. "Coffee, senor? Just how you asked."

CHAPTER 23

▼

Stone's Throw was aptly named. Sitting high atop the hill behind the house, Addie could almost touch the Boston skyline to the right and the broadcast tower on the Great Blue Hill on the left. It must have had something to do with air currents, light refraction across the water or something, but even though the city was almost 20 miles away, here on Marla's little private island, Addie had the overwhelming urge to wrap a message around a stone and hurl it across to the now electrified city, certain it would find its mark.

Up and around well before the rest of the odd assortment that comprised the household in the aftermath of last night's bizarre little party, Addie wanted to have the time to commune with The Great Spirit in peace and quiet away from the madness that would surely surround her later in the day. The fringed buckskin dress that she'd chosen for March was not as warm as she'd expected it to be. And the moccasins. They made her bare feet feel as though they were encased in clammy mud. The ancestors, hers, Walter's, whatever - Walter's in a physical sense, hers in a spiritual - must have worn something under the them or at least under the buckskin, because it was incredibly drafty and quite damp and clingy. Some sort of cotton, perhaps. When was Polar Fleece invented? Was Polar Fleece a natural fiber? Did the indigenous peoples have Polar Fleece? That was something she really should check. She would want to display historically accurate costumes in the museum and felt it important to walk a mile in the dress or moccasins of her ancestors before she did so. Polar Fleece actually would be a quite acceptable lining for her buckskin and quite an acceptable mantra for her early morning meditation. Polar Fleece. A lovely rhythmical sound. All those l's and vowels rolling around in her mouth. Polar Fleece. Polar Fleece. Greeting the sunrise. Polar Fleece. Good morning, sun.

> Polar Fleece.
> May warfare cease.
> Help me to save

What could she rhyme with fleece? Lease? Help me renew my lease? Help me renew my lease with my niece? Help me renew my lease with my niece on the land in New Jersey and bring us peace. No. no. Geese? Perhaps, perhaps.

She was deep into it, teetering just on the brink of consciousness, this close to transcending this valley of tears when she was jarred awake. One voice was probably human; the other perhaps animal, perhaps feline, perhaps extraterrestrial. The chorus of dueling shrieks, catcalls and yelps was impossible to identify. Of course. Who else could it be? The madwoman, flaming face as florid a red as the lettering on the pebble filled Diet Coke can she waved wildly at her poor victim. One of the geese? Had she called unto their spirit? No. Not a goose. The creature, the innocent child of the universe of the Great White Father, hissing, spitting, baring his enormous tongue threateningly at squat little Lulu Noone who had decided to make it her mission to shepherd the young swan back into the water. For a woman who claimed to be an artist, who claimed to be able to see the world through the trained eyes of a seeker of beauty and composition, she lacked even the most rudimentary sense of the symmetry and significance of the young brown swan leaving the water, torn between his desire for the safety and security of his pond and his parents and the freedom of his solitary adventure in the wider world. Even if that wider world was merely the lawn behind Stone's Throw. Wailing and flailing the Diet Coke can, only intermittently intimidated by the surprisingly hefty bird's hissed recriminations, Lulu Noone huffed and puffed her wobbly body up and down the bank of the little pond behind the abandoned caretaker's cottage.

Addie could bear it no longer. Fleet of foot thanks to the clammy moccasins which had adhered to and molded to the shape of her feet, she stealthily made her way down the hillside towards the deranged swan beater.

"Leave that poor creature alone! He's not bothering you. Put that can down!"

"He belongs in the water. Waterfowl belong in the water. We must save him. This is for his own good. He doesn't understand. He's been exposed to too much radiation from that TV station," she pumped her plump doughy arms in the general direction of up. "And he's lost his natural instinct. His compass has been tampered with. There are satellites all over the place here you know. They fly over here all the time. They say that's a TV tower. Right. We know what it is. It's for the satellites. The satellites use it to take their bearings. Great Blue Hill. That's what they say. Going Back Home. That's what they want to do. Be sure their satellites can find their way back home. And we fall for it." She took in a gulp of air. "They're watching us now. They beam things. They're experimenting with us. Experimenting with him." By now, the poor swan lay exhausted on a patch of dry grass. "He needs to be back in the water. The rays can't get to his brain when he's in the water. We've got to save him. Help me, please."

The swan rose to a squat on the grass and stared pleading at Addie.

"It is a TV tower. What are you saying? What do you think it is?"

"That's what they'd like us to believe. TV tower. My foot. Like they use all those cans and bottles we recycle. Like they landed a man on the moon. Like they really discontinued Conglomotron neon tubing number 144MB. It's a great big hoax. I wasn't born yesterday, you know. I'm on to them. They're all cheats and liars."

Addie surprised herself by actually feeling some genuine interest in what this nut was saying. Her Native American sensibility flashed to an image of a once pristine forest primeval bulging with festering mounds of garbage and bottles and CD ROMS and cans not unlike the one Miss Lulu Noone had been brandishing at this docile creature. OK, maybe not so docile, but he had been provoked.

"Is it really true? About those cans and bottles?"

"It's all a scam. Don't you get it?" The redness in her cheeks calmed somewhat as she inhaled purposefully a few times and assumed the air of the tutor instructing the ignorant.

"I'm surprised really that a well educated woman like yourself, a well informed woman, a woman in touch with the earth and the synergy of the world would allow herself to be taken in by their lies."

The cygnet took advantage of this distraction to make his move. He pivoted and flapped the huge gray trapezoids that were his feet and in a matter of seconds had slipped silently into the water. The huge feet extending behind him seemed to elongate his neck as he stretched and dipped and drank the scummy familiar water. Each woman took the swan's immersion as her own personal victory. Addie had saved him from a Coke can wielding conspiracy theorist; Lulu had prevented him from further exposure to the beamed experimental rays.

"What about you? Are you subject to the rays from the satellites?" Addie tried valiantly to keep her voice from betraying any trace of her skepticism. "Do you need to be on water or the mother ship or something?"

"No. Of course not." Lulu Noone smiled patronizingly at the unenlightened. She reached into the mop of greasy Auburn curls that spiked from every direction on her head and unpinned a rectangle of fuzzy tangerine colored cloth, cloth that was colored as if to be camouflaged within her tresses. She fingered the material knowingly, gauging its worth. "This is all we need. Nothing can get through it. It's non-woven, colorfast, non-pilling and machine washable. Its molecular structure bounces anything right back at them. They can't touch me through this stuff." Her smug little smile crinkled the crow's feet around her eyes. She giggled girlishly. "If Superman could have had this, the Kryptonite could never have gotten him."

Addie was intrigued. She walked closer to examine this close to invisible shield that Lulu Noone was using to protect herself from the malevolent interplanetary rays beamed around the hemisphere by unnamed satellites. It looked familiar. She hesitantly brought it to her face and sniffed, fearful that she might inadvertently inhale a bodily fluid emitted by this red and white spotted lump of protoplasm.

"I've seen this before. It seems so familiar. But, I just can't place it." She turned it over once, twice then again. "It's … yes, it's, could it be? Yes, it's Polar Fleece."

The two women, united now by the common Polar Fleece thread that bound them, were now able to sublimate their differences and process their feelings about the unbelievable night they had spent. Each had been assigned a room in which to pass the night; each had occupied a room which had been made up room for a participant in the matrix regression therapy workshop; each had been offered but declined to wear freshly laundered and ironed sleep wear which matched the sheets on their respective beds. Neither of the nightgowns was made of Polar Fleece. If hers had been, perhaps Lulu would have worn it simply for protection. The apricot front button gown hung on the door of the apricot room; the lavender linen tailored pajamas in the lavender room. Each woman, for her own private reason, had preferred to sleep in her own clothes ready, if necessary, to leave this place at a moment's notice. Sleep was really not what either of them did. Lulu lay fully clothed on the made bed waiting for daylight. Addie had sat up in a chair watching her husband, Walter, sleep the sleep of the innocent, snoring and sputtering and scratching at the same regular intervals he snored and sputtered and scratched in his own bed on Commonwealth Avenue. Well before dawn, they were both ready to face the world and be the first to leave Marla's little island. Addie had slipped away unnoticed by Walter. Lulu had slipped away unnoticed by anyone except perhaps the observers monitoring the surveillance images beamed back from the orbiting satellites. Neither had expected the other, but here they were. The swan having paddled well out of range of any Diet Coke can and Addie's solitary morning meditation irreparably interrupted, the two women faced one another with nothing to talk about but last night.

"It was that little girl you know. I don't blame her one bit. I could have done it myself, but it was that little girl."

"Little girl?" Addie truly didn't know what Lulu was talking about.

"Pam. Fuller Arden's little girlfriend. She's the one. She's the one who wanted to kill Jack Trumpet. Like I said, I don't blame her a bit. The man's a snake. I could kill him myself." She sidled up to Addie and wrapped a pudgy little arm around her shoulder. "He's the one responsible for everything you know. He's the one", she whispered. "It was his wife who was killed. Nobody tried to kill Mr. Trumpet. Whatever are you talking about?" Addie had stopped even bothering to pay attention to the investigatory proceedings once she realized she would be excluded from Bomatumbi Mabata's workshop.

"Don't you listen? Don't you pay attention at all?" Lulu never had any patience with a pupil who wasn't even trying. "Didn't you hear what Trumpet said last night?"

Addie had heard quite a few things, most of which had not been intended for her ears, so she quite politely, disregarded them. She stared blankly at Miss Noone.

"She was sitting in *his* seat. That was *his* soup", Lulu Noon announced to her feathered friend.

"It was gazpacho."

"Gazpacho, then. The fact is that *he* was the intended victim. Not Mrs. Trumpet. She only sat there because of the candlelight or something. It reflected badly on her plastic surgery. Eye lifts? Cheek implants? What?"

"You're asking me?" Addie was now the impatient one. "You're the one telling the story, not me."

"The fact remains that *he* not Mrs. Trumpet was the intended victim. He did something totally out of character. He gave up something for someone else. It was probably the first time in his life that he did something for nothing."

Addie felt the need to defend her choice of guests whom she introduced into the club.

"Actually, it was Walter and I who brought them over here last night. I don't know her very well, but he's quite lovely, really, and generous. I'm not sure how you can say he's never done anything for anyone. They're making a very generous contribution to a little project I'm working on," she proudly fluffed her buckskin fringe "And I thought that since they're new to the area it would be nice to introduce them around. Besides," she paused. "Giving up his seat is nothing. That hardly counts. She is, or ... was his wife, after all. People do things for their wives and husbands all the time without expecting something in return. Have you ever been married?"

"Not in this lifetime honey." Lulu smiled a knowing smile. Almost a smirk. She liked to give the impression of one who's dodged the bullet more times than she'd like to recall, while in fact a bullet had never even been fired in her direction. "And, take my word for it, not in this lifetime would this guy, this Trumpet, do something for nothing. He's corporate America. Corporate America. The very essence of corruption. It was his company that staged that whole," she did that finger wiggle quotation mark thing, "moon landing charade."

"Charade?" Addie had watched the moon landing on TV along with the rest of America. Her face apparently betrayed her incredulity.

"You didn't fall for that did you?"

"Well, yes or ... I mean no ... I mean I guess. But, it wasn't a charade. I saw it myself."

"It was brilliantly staged but not quite brilliantly enough for someone like me. I could spot their mistakes immediately." She was smug; she was superior; and now, she was going to instruct naïve little Addie on the finer points of the conspiracy.

"Like I told Neon Jimmy it was all a hoax. Those Conglomotron engines on the rockets couldn't even get through the radiation shield. They never could have even gotten as far as the moon, so how could they land there? Then, to cover their billion dollar asses, they cooked up this scam. Had to make it look to the taxpayers that the bucks they were spending were for something. So, they staged this "landing" at Area 51 and everyone fell for it." Her little beady eyes narrowed to two slits above her crinkled nose. "Almost everyone, that is." She looked first over one shoulder, then the other. Seeing no eavesdroppers, she continued. "But, they found out and now I'm being punished for what I know."

"Who's punishing you?" Addie was beginning to fear that she could possibly believe this woman. She was starting to make sense.

"Conglomotron. Who else? They discontinued my neon tubing, the tubing I use for my art. I need that. My art needs that." Her poor rosacia red face was beginning to flare. "So that's the punishment they chose for me". She sighed. "Discontinue my tubing. Hit em where it hurts, huh?"

"This was Mr. Trumpet's doing?" Addie was becoming engrossed in this story.

"Of course, he's Conglomotron. He's a snake. He has no heart."

Addie felt the need to defend the animal kingdom. She was planning to include a section in the museum that displayed animals which could have been found in and around the natural habitat of her people. She felt quite knowledgeable to speak. "Snakes actually have hearts. If you'd said he was a rock or say a fungus, they don't have hearts, but snakes do. Snakes have hearts. Snakes are cold blooded. You could say he's a snake; he's cold blooded. But, if you're talking hearts, yes they have hearts."

"Listen to me, the man's no good. Wait until you hear what he did to our little murderess. You'll understand then."

"Murderess?"

"You didn't notice her getting drinks for people, for the Trumpets, offering to get hors d'oeuvres for them, hanging around the table, leaning over what should have been Trumpet's soup with that big green dress of hers obscuring what she was doing. You didn't notice that?"

"No." Addie felt like a fool. "No, I didn't notice a thing".

"She had plenty of time to slip her something into her soup."

"Gazpacho. But why? Why would that lovely quiet little Pam want to kill Barbie Lee Trumpet?"

"I told you. It's not Barbie Lee. It's Jack. It's Jack. Barbie Lee just happened to move to his seat at the last minute." Lulu was becoming exasperated. "You really *don't* listen do you?"

"All right. Then why would she want to kill Jack Trumpet?"

"Her father."

"Her father?"

"Her father. Jack Trumpet and his evil empire, Conglomotron ruined her father's life and, by extension, her mother's and hers."

Addie's eyes asked her instructor to continue.

"Her father's outfit had been in line to be acquired by Conglomotron and they welched."

"Was it bioinformatics? Telecommunications?

"Emus."

"Emus?"

"Emus. And when Conglomotron welched, dad walked. No one ever saw him again. Poor kid, the old man sank every last buck into those stupid animals and Trumpet welched. Then the old man shot himself or something. Can you blame little Pam? And, Fuller is so gah gah over her, he'd help her in a minute."

"Fuller is conducting the investigation until the police can get here."

"Sure he is. And what better way to obscure the evidence against his girlfriend than to" she again did her favorite little finger quotation marks "investigate"?

"You can't possibly be serious?" Addie said.

"Listen, you investigate here, smear a few fingerprints there, track around the crime scene a little. Believe me, it can be done. It was done to me. I know that for a fact."

"Lulu Noone. That's preposterous. That's not evidence that she did anything. You can't believe that that darling little girl is responsible for Mrs. Trumpet's death. Why, someone could easily create a scenario where *you're* the one who did it."

Suddenly, without warning, from an unseen grassy knoll behind them, a hail of buckshot rang out. Addie and Lulu, without thinking embraced and clung to one another, hearts pounding. The bay and rush of Daisey the Retriever was followed by the footsteps of Acumulada, a smoking shotgun draped across her arm.

"Buenos Dias, senoras". She smiled her golden smile. "Mrs. Marla wants a little something for the Bomatumbi visitors tonight.

*   *   *   *

PHEASANT

Pluck the bird and be careful not to tear the skin. Draw, wipe but do not wash. Truss like any other foul. Rub the outside with olive oil and fasten strips of salt pork to the breast and thighs. Roast at 400 degrees basting every five minutes until browned about 35 minutes.

CHAPTER 24

▼

"We'll never get away with this. They'll find out." Pam was practically in tears.

Fuller tenderly embraced his fiancee. "There's no way anyone will know. They certainly won't hear it from me."

"I know you didn't want to do this. I know you let me talk you into it. I'm sorry. I'm so sorry. Especially if we get caught. You'll be ruined."

Pam was especially beautiful this morning. Her flawless skin, round innocent eyes, teeth just crooked enough to be adorable all added up to the many reasons he'd fallen in love with her and why she had made it to become the first runner up in the audition for Dallas Cowboy Cheerleaders. She would make a beautiful bride. His bride. And, once they were married and settled in the remodeled carriage house on Fuller's family estate, Pam could really come into her own. If this law enforcement thing didn't work out in the long term, he'd eventually be willing to take his place in the family business. It was, after all, almost preordained. Pam could then assume her rightful place with the young wives of his classmates, join the Junior League, host charity parties, maybe get involved in the League of Women Voters and work for a good Republican candidate. Marla would take her under her wing, teach her how to cook, how to gold leaf and introduce her around. Fuller was sure he could count on Marla to give Pam that last little polish that she needed to let the real Pammy Wammy shine through. She could put this emu business with her father behind her and carve out a new life for herself with him.

"Nobody had a gun to my head. I did it because I wanted to. If anything, I should be apologizing to you. What about your reputation?" he smiled, teasing her. "Mrs. Arden?"

Pam giggled the bubbly little giggle he loved and kissed him lightly on the nose.

"It sounds quiet out there now. Maybe one of us should look to see if the coast is clear. Then you can go back to your room and no one will find out."

Fuller was suddenly feeling less inclined to leave. The morning sun filtered through the white plantation shutters and enticingly illuminated her silhouette through the sheer white linen of her virginal high button nightgown as she stood listening at the door. That high button nightgown had been intended for someone in the matrix regression workshop, but no one would be able to fill it out the way his little Pam had last night. The thought of their night together and the prospect of sticking around for a little more this morning suppressed some of his inhibitions.

"Would it really be so bad if we got caught? Who's to catch us anyway? Is someone going to come in here? What are we worried about? We are, after all, engaged."

"I think you should go, Fully. We'll have plenty of time later", she whispered as she gently stole one little nibble on his earlobe. "I promise."

"Coffee is ready downstairs!!" It was Acumulada in the hall.

"Too late. Everyone must be up already. We'll have to wait." Pam was beginning to panic.

"I can't wait. I'm supposed to be conducting this investigation". Fuller's inhibitions were back in working order.

"But, someone will see you leave. They'll know you spent the night. I feel so guilty. They'll think I'm a slut. Oh, please, Fully, wait until the coast is clear. Please. Don't leave now. Please."

Fuller pulled the pair of cane backed chairs over to the door. "Let's sit here and listen." He examined the door. "Wonder if this keyhole is operational. Love to be able to see what's going on in the hall."

"Here, let me take a look". Pam wriggled and writhed and twisted and turned inside her linen nightgown in an effort to create some sort of periscopic vision through the long unused keyhole. Her gyrations were almost enough for Fuller to consider once more throwing in the towel on the investigation and throwing her back to bed, but he, through superhuman strength, resisted. Inhibitions once again reigned.

"We're just going to have to sit here and listen. Be very quiet and listen. No funny moves; no heavy breathing. Just sit here and listen."

Pam was suddenly lost deep in thought. "Illicit love can be a terrible, hurtin' thing."

"Will you stop it. We're not illicit. We're engaged."

"I wasn't talking about us, Fully, I meant Florence Bainbridge and Ledge Stone. They say she killed him. Killed him and stuffed him into the trunk of her car. Her Bentley. I've never even seen a Bentley. Have you?"

"Who says this? Who have you been talking to?"

"That skinny one. The one with the plastic cigarette. Loretta? The doctor's wife."

"Lucretia. Lucretia Franklin. What did she say?"

"Florence and Ledge Stone", she whispered conspiratorily, "He was still legally married to Marla at the time, were carrying on. She wanted him to leave and things weren't moving fast enough for her, so, in a fit of passion, she killed him and stuffed him into the trunk of her car." Pam leaned even closer to Fuller revealing that she'd opened all but one of the buttons on her high button night-gown. "Now, Lucretia says Florence has killed again."

"Barbie Lee Trumpet?? Why on earth would Florence want to kill Barbie Lee Trumpet?"

"Just to make Marla look bad. To spoil her party. So Marla wouldn't get that show they were talking about with Barbie Lee." She shrugged. "Who knows? Apparently, Florence was real deep in love with Ledge and Marla gave everyone a real hard time about them getting together. Just wouldn't let go. So, for Florence now is just payback time." Pam read the look on Fuller's face. "At least that's what she told me."

"That makes no sense whatsoever. If anyone would have wanted to kill Ledge it would have been Everett. He is, after all, the cuckold."

"Cuckold." Her little giggle escaped her lips. "It sounds like something Daddy did to the emus."

"Cuckold. It's a man whose wife has been unfaithful."

"You don't have to be critical of me just because my vocabulary isn't as good as yours." Pam bristled.

"Don't be petulant, honey."

"Don't you call me something that I don't know what it is".

Fuller was sorry he'd started this, but was not about to drop it. "Would you prefer 'bitchy'?"

"Is that what you think? Is that what you think I am? Bitchy? Bitchy? I'll show you bitchy. You and all your fancy friends who never even heard of a double wide, I'll show you bitchy."

She stood and was just about to open the door to storm out of the room when she realized she was stuck here, at least for the time being. The momentary interruption gave her just enough time to reconsider her petulant bitchiness. She approached Fuller who was relishing the apology he knew he was about to receive.

"I'm sorry, hon. I guess I was being a little petulant." She sighed. "Heck, I was being a bitch." She cocked her head and peeked at him. "Forgive me?"

That was enough for Fuller. He grinned his best perfect American tooth grin. "Oh, baby. You know I do. Come back over here." He patted his lap, but Pam instead returned to the cane chair beside his. She was all business. She wanted more information; she wanted to fill in the blanks left in the story Lucretia had told her.

"Listen, Fully, if Florence didn't do it, who do you think did? You must have some ideas. You're the quarterback on this team, aren't you? Least for now?"

"Well, if you're talking about Ledge's murder, it certainly wasn't Florence. Like I said Everett is the cuckold. That's c-u-c-k-o-l-d."

Pam slapped his hand playfully.

Fuller continued in what he hoped was his official police department tone, "Authorities are seeking members of a Colombian drug cartel for that murder. The investigation is still open. The Bainbridge's son, Scott, was one suspect; Everett was another. But, both of them were completely cleared on that one. Scott was traveling somewhere in Asia and Everett was on a business trip in Istanbul when Ledge was murdered. The Conglomotron executives he met with there swore he was with them for several days."

Pam was beginning to feel a little petulance welling up in her throat but managed to repress it. "Everett Bainbridge does business with Conglomotron?? Does that man have everyone on his payroll?"

"Everett sold his company to Conglomotron. That's what the trip to Istanbul was all about. With the merger and acquisition, they needed to streamline the staff, reduce duplication on the executive level and all that." Pam interrupted, "Sure, they had to fire most of the people in Bainbridge's company. So there'd be enough money for the fat cats to split up. I wonder how many of them flipped out and left their families high and dry?"

Fuller was hoping this conversation was not going to deteriorate into yet another indictment of the evils of corporate America and the injustice the poor and downtrodden had to endure. He tried to sound matter-of-fact. "It was a huge deal. Made all the papers. He made a killing. He had this little medical devices company that Conglomotron acquired for many hundred of millions and Everett Bainbridge retired a very rich guy."

"So, Conglomotron bought *his* company and not my daddy's. Is that justice? I ask you. Is that justice?"

"Your daddy had an emu ranch, honey. Everett Bainbridge had a company that had international patents on minimally invasive surgical devices." He tried to sound kind. "There's a big difference."

"Maybe. So, who do you think did it to Barbie Lee? Was it Everett with a minimally invasive instrument?"

"I think, as everyone does, that Barbie Lee was simply in the wrong place at the wrong time. An innocent victim of violence intended for her husband."

"So, who? Come on!!"

Fuller paused. He hated to say it, but, Pam, after all, was going to be his wife and if he couldn't be forthright with her, with whom could he be?

"He's a nice guy and it's not official, but all clues lead to", he paused for effect. "Everett Bainbridge, Everett, of course, targeting Jack Trumpet and inadvertently killing Mrs. Trumpet."

"Why?"

"Everett's still a young man. He's got quite a few good years ahead of him and he's retired, doing nothing but packing and unpacking. His days are marked by whether or not they're just coming back from a vacation or getting ready to leave on one. If they're home for any length of time, it's only so Florence can have a tuck or nip or implant so she can look good at the next charity ball. That's not what this guy had planned on for his retirement. He doesn't even like golf."

"What has that got to do with Jack Trumpet?" Pam was beginning to feel that Fuller was being purposely obtuse, just to annoy her.

It wasn't exactly a sigh, but an extended exhale that carried Fuller's next words. "There was a clause. There is a clause. There is a clause in the acquisition contract. In the event of a change in the upper echelons of management of Conglomotron within the first five years after the acquisition, the seller, in this case, Everett, has the right to nullify the acquisition, retaining for himself the prorated funds equal to an amount which would have been paid during the five year period had the change in management not occurred."

Pam was not certain that Fuller was trying to annoy her, but he could be. "English please."

"OK. If Trumpet were to die, Everett could get his company back and still keep a big chunk of change."

"So, he could go back to work and not have to go to Indonesia with Florence all the time? That seals it. He definitely did it. He's pretty creepy anyway. And, why did he take her back anyway after that Ledge fiasco?"

"Why not? It's not like he had a job to go to during the day. Like I said, he doesn't even golf."

"A mucho buenos dias to the honeymooners." Without the slightest warning the French window had flown open and there, big as life in her soundless Rebok sneakers, Acumulada stood. "I brought for you the fresh towels. It was a long night, no?"

"Ms. Candelario. I just got here. Just wanted to check on Pam. After last night and all. You know how it is." Fuller's words spilled out one on top of the other.

"Mr. Arden Fuller, we got some cameras in this house. I show you. You be finding what I show you very, very interesting. You come with me. Si?"

Poor Pam's heart sank. She'd been caught.

CHAPTER 25

▼

From the lawn surrounding the paddock to the caretaker's cottage was about a nine iron shot. Patrick the blind man had been an adequate high school athlete. That was, of course, when he was in high school and before he had been stricken with this damn PND and before his back gave out and his neck and jaw had started acting up and before he began to show the early symptoms of restless leg syndrome. That was when he had teenage muscles which easily remembered what that were taught. Teenage muscles were immune to the aches and pains inherent in the mature adult. Mature adults whose muscles had learned the game in high school or before were the ones who were able to excel on the links or the rinks or the fields. Patrick's sport of choice in high school had been ice dancing and it was a bit of a stretch to figure out how skills like a back outside edge triple twizzle were applicable to golf. He could, though, try. He had, after all, spent a small fortune for a full set of Callaways, the top of the line bag and all the bells and whistles that went with them.

It looked like he had an unexpectedly free morning over here at Stone's Throw and maybe even longer. Who knew how long it would be before they were sprung. Might as well take advantage of it. Despite last night's freak storm, spring was almost here, at least on the calendar. All the golf courses were already open. Some of them hadn't ever closed.

This was going to be the year of golf. This was the year Patrick the blind man would take some time for himself and master the game. This was the year Patrick the blind man would let his nephew Jason take over a little bit of responsibility for the store. It was time for Patrick the blind man to start to stop and smell the roses. Marla rarely invited him to play. Actually, Marla had never invited him to play. In the last couple of years, Marla rarely had the time to play. But, when she did, it was with someone other than Patrick. It would have been humiliating for him to play with Marla. It was pretty much humiliating for anyone to play with Marla. She was a natural. She'd been playing since old Waldo Saltonstall had brought her around the course with him almost as soon as she could walk. Waldo had never had a son, so he decided to impart all that father-to-son handed-down knowledge to his daughter. Marla hit the ball a country mile and straight. If she played twice a year it was a lot and yet, every time she went out, after a bucket on the practice tee, she parred just about every hole. She was a natural. Not everyone was. Some people had to learn and work at it. Patrick had promised himself that he would and could. This year, golf would be something he and Marla could share. He would have more time and she would have more money.

Now, with Barbie Lee unfortunately deceased, Marla could do the TV show for Trumpet by herself. A solo act. On her own. Singular. A singular sensation. It would be a better program with just Marla. She'd be paid the same and maybe drop some of these nickel and dime, penny ante, small time, bush league projects that consumed so much of her time. Birdsong identification; jam and jelly workshops, gold leafing. She didn't need those people here in her house. She didn't need gold leafing students here at Stone's Throw. It's no wonder the bridge gave out. With all the traffic that had been coming over back and forth across that bridge since she started these courses, it's a miracle it didn't just fall in on its own without that storm last night.

She could drop those cockamamie classes and concentrate on making some real money, some real simoleans, some do re mi in television, the boob tube, the idiot box. That's where she belonged – tinsel town. Once she hit it big and became a household name, instantly recognizable in every restaurant in New York, Patrick could maybe really give Jason some responsibility and start distancing himself from the blind business for once and for all. Squiring a big celebrity around town could easily become a full-time job for a guy with Patrick's particular skill set. He would, of course, need some clothes. What he had for these people at The Club was OK. But, for television?? No. They'd never do. He'd need to fashion his look around someone else, someone with flair. Flair was what we're talking about. That Jack Trumpet. Now, he had flair; he knew how to dress. Loved that look.

Patrick chose a ball from the wire bucket at his feet and carefully placed it on a tee. He then pondered the clubs in his leather bag. This was the one. This was the one he'd use. If a balloon sculptor created a golf club, this is what it would look like. A six foot long yellow shaft topping an over-sized candy apple red candy apple, gleaming in the morning sun. Bozo could easily have been the spokesman for this club. Perfect. It had been custom made for him by Leo Martin over at the pro shop. Patrick addressed the ball, trying to remember every lesson he'd taken. Head down, knees relaxed, right elbow straight, shoulders down, butt out. He brought the club back and swung. He had never seen anything so beautiful. It soared, a perfect little white planet orbiting the paddock of Stone's Throw. It was an extremely beautiful sight until the crash. It made a direct hit on the third window from the left of the although presently uninhabited, hardly what one would consider abandoned, caretaker's cottage. The shattering glass was enough to wake the dead.

Although he hadn't exactly been dead, Walter Coolidge *was* awakened and emerged from the caretaker's cottage

"Good God, man! What are you? Blind? What do you think you're doing?" He strode angrily towards the scene of Patrick's crime, his dangling eyeglasses bouncing from the cord around his neck, waving his ivory topped walking stick threateningly over his head.

"Oh, Walter. Boy. Wow. Gee. I'm so sorry. I didn't have any idea. Wow. I guess I really hit that one." He was contrite. "I just came out here to chase this little white ball around and, jeez, look what happened. Who put that window there? Wow. Jeez. I hope I didn't cause anyone any *pane*." His laugh was bordering on pathetic.

"Don't you have any control over your shots? What do you think you're doing? Have you got any idea where the ball is going? You can't just come out here and hit golf balls without knowing what you're doing. Are you crazy? You could have killed someone."

"Jeez, I hope I didn't. Are you all right? Are you alone?"

"Yes, I'm all right and yes I'm alone. For the moment. I think my wife might be out here somewhere, though. She usually does her morning mediation from a high point in the east. She could be around any of these knolls. God only knows -you could have killed her." As he said the words, for the tiniest nanosecond, Walter wondered what it would be like if Patrick *had* killed Addie. What it would be like to be a widower, what it would be like to be alone the way Jack Trumpet was alone this morning. Peace, quiet, no Native Americans living in their garage apartment, no morning scramble to figure out which way was east. He brushed these thoughts from his mind as quickly as they'd rushed in.

"No, no. That's the only ball I hit. I didn't hit any others. That's the only one. I didn't kill anyone. I'm sure of it. I just know it. I'm really sure."

Walter reached for the bright red driver in Patrick's hand. "What is this? Do you call this a golf club?"

"It is actually. It's a new custom made driver. Leo Martin made it for me. He uses one. It increases your distance by 35%. That's over a third."

"Yuh", Walter snorted. "Like those clubs Conglomotron makes. Who ever heard of golf clubs made of space age plastic? No wonder that guy killed his wife with one. They're all gimmicks. In my day, a golf club was a golf club. Woods were made of wood. Amazing, huh? And irons were made of iron. We walked the course with a caddy and hit the ball straight, godammit, and we knew where it was going. They didn't sell golf clubs to people who didn't know what they were doing."

"I'm really sorry, Walter. It was an accident, I assure you. Maybe I should have yelled 'fore' or 'three' or, if I'd known it was you in that cottage 'five'. Heh, heh." His goofy laugh was squeezed out of the bellows he'd made of his body by hinging at the waist and shrugging his shoulders. All those years of ice dancing had left him with an unusually agile spine.

"Well, I guess it was an accident. Just try to be more careful, huh? Maybe use some of those wiffle balls until you have a little more control over where it's going, hey, old man?"

Old man? Patrick took this as a sign he'd been forgiven. That he'd been reaccepted into the inner circle. Old man. There was hardly a kinder term of endearment that one could expect from Walter Coolidge. Old man. Yes. He was forgiven. Yes. He would try to improve. He would do more than try, he *would* improve. Maybe someday, Walter would invite him to play golf with him. Maybe.

"Listen, Patrick, put that confounded thing down and come with me to find my wife. I'm sure she's around here somewhere. Fuller wants everyone in the library this morning and I don't want Addie to miss it."

The two men, the two old men, headed across the lawn towards the paddock. Neither had thrown his arm over the other's shoulder. It was hardly the beginning of a beautiful friendship, but, it had potential.

"What a mess. What a calamity. What a fiasco. That poor woman. Who could have done it?"

Walter Coolidge was not an outspoken man. He'd used up virtually all of his emotional outburst quota in response to Patrick's errant golf ball through the window. He thought carefully now before he spoke.

"I hate to say it, but, there's only one person who would benefit from that woman's demise. Only one. Only one who had access to her soup."

"It was gazpacho".

"Whatever." He continued, "That woman, I'm afraid, was our hostess."

Patrick stopped dead in his tracks. "No. I demand that you retract that statement. Marla could never have done anything like that. There's not a murderous bone in her body."

"Have you ever seen her cook a live lobster? She is merciless."

STEAMED LOBSTER

In a large kettle containing 3 inches of boiling water, add 2 Tablespoons salt. Plunge lobster in head first. Cover. Reduce heat just enough to maintain boiling point and steam lobsters for 17 minutes for one pound; 18 to 20 minutes for 1 ¼ pounds. Remove from kettle and place on its back. Cut lobster from head to tail. Spread open and remove intestinal vein and small sac just below the head. Serve with lemon and drawn butter.

Patrick needed to convince himself that Marla was not the killer. He also needed to erase from his mind the image of his beloved Marla dispassionately chopping the head off that chicken last Friday afternoon. Anyone who could do that …

"Is Fuller sure it was murder? Not an accident?"

"Trumpet is sure it's an accident in a manner of speaking. He's convinced someone had it in for him and that someone poisoned the soup he was supposed to eat. He changed seats with his wife and she ate it – the poison meant for him".

"Gazpacho." Patrick continued, "If it really was Trumpet who was the intended victim, it had to have been that man, that wife murderer. He's the one with a record and besides," he lowered his voice almost to a whisper, "he's a minority."

As the two men rounded the next bend in the path and approached the apple orchard, they came face to face with her. Acumulada, juggling a Titelist 4 came far too close to Patrick's face for his comfort. "He was acquitted."

CHAPTER 26

▼

They assembled promptly at 11 in the library, most of them anyway. Last night's costumes, for the most part, did not succeed as daywear. Florence's and Lucretia's sequins which looked particularly silly in daylight were counter-balanced nicely by Addie's buckskin and Lulu Noone's rumpled whatever it was. Patrick and Marla were the only ones who had the luxury of a total change of clothes. Acumulada wore what could have been a fresh pink uniform – she had dozens – or it could have been the same one she'd been wearing earlier this morning before she changed for the *"Guiding Light"* at 10. It was, in fact, Acumulada who had requested that the meeting be scheduled for 11. When she realized it was Sunday and she would miss her soap even if they had electricity, she simply changed into a Versace outfit and spent the better part of an hour imagining what Alan Spaulding and Phillip and Reva and Josh would be doing today.

Walter Coolidge arrived and found a seat next to his new-found friend. Walter's striped goatee bobbed almost imperceptibly up and down as he tried to silently convey to Patrick his sympathy that his beloved, his dear sweet Marla, should be involved in such a fiasco. Patrick welcomed the company but needed little of his sympathy. There was nothing to be sympathetic about. Once the police (the real police) got here and arrested P.D. Quinn, this whole thing would be over and Marla could get her TV career in gear. Yeah, he thought, thanks for the sympathy, old man, but, no thanks. Where was the murderer, anyway? Maybe Fuller had already locked him up.

Fuller, Pam by his side, took his place in front of the fireplace. This was his moment in the sun. This was his investigation and he had the goods on the killer, partly because of his keen police skills and partly because of an astutely observant uncannily perceptive informant.

"Well, we need just a few more people to arrive and then we can begin."

From deep in the hallway, behind the heavy oak door, the fracas could be clearly heard by Acumulada as well as those with hearing which registered in the normal range.

"You'll need more than a doctor 'fore I get through with you, yousummbitch. I know what you up to. You try to frame P.D., I'll show you what happens to a shit who tries to frame P.D. You'll be sorry you mutha ever jumped your ole man."

The scuffle had progressed down the hall and had spilled into the library. Fists and arms and legs and heads bumped into the walls and into each other. Dr. Franklin, Old Mr. Young and P.D. Quinn had passed the point when words would be effective to settle their dispute. The two old white guys were doing surprisingly well against the heavily muscled, black former ballplayer. Arthritis can be crippling.

"Oh, my God. Fuller, do something!!" Pam looked to be on the brink of hysteria.

"All right you guys, break it up, break it up. That's enough. Knock it off." All those seasons of kayaking had created a pretty impressive upper body that Fuller was now inserting into the fray. "What's going on?"

"He started it. That man is crazy. I never did a thing to him. He started it." Old Mr. Young, who'd only taken a few hits, was rising and brushing himself off. "He seems to think one of my clients was somehow involved in his indictment. He'll see what it means to be involved with my firm once we're back home." He turned to his assailant. "You'll be hearing from Young, Young and Silverberg, my good man, and after you do, you can plan to be parted from every dime you have salted away here or anywhere on earth. You'll be very sorry you ever attacked Seymour Young."

Dr. Franklin looked considerably worse than Old Mr. Young. "Seymour, look I want to check you over. You need to be checked. You took quite a few hits back there. Let me give you a once over."

"Not now. There'll be plenty of time for a full examination with a full team of specialists once we're back in town. This animal, this murderer will pay and pay damn good for this."

"I was acquited. You know that."

"Gentlemen, gentlemen, please." Marla needed to rein in some of the bedlam that was overtaking her house. One word from her did the trick.

Reluctantly, the three teen-agers in old men's bodies shuffled and skulked, hangdog, into the library.

That little interruption dealt with, Fuller could resume his introduction. But, wait. There was still one person missing. Jack Trumpet, the bereaved widower. He had been waiting upstairs, waiting for all the suspects to fill the library, waiting to face the one or ones responsible for his attempted assassination. Waiting to face the one or ones who had taken from him his beloved Barbie Lee. He was here now. Somewhere in this room was the killer.

The unexpected pajama party last night had left Jack Trumpet a little off kilter this morning. His clothes had survived nicely because he had, as usual, slept in the nude. In addition to sleeping in the buff, he also enjoyed his coffee au naturel, a fact a startled Acumulada learned when she made her rounds to clear the rooms. The red Speedo he'd appeared in earlier seemed positively modest compared with the sight with which she'd been greeted today. His clothes did look fine. It was the rest of him that had not passed the night unscathed. His hair plugs had apparently been harvested from the back of his neck and were a dramatically different color than the sparse hair which continued to sprout unassisted from his head. The plugs were so dramatically different in color – pure white – that they required a daily application of Roux Fancifull shampoo-in-color to even the tones and soften the equator which circled his skull marking the zone of inserted plugs and his God-given hair. It would be several months before the doctor could give him the go ahead to use permanent hair color on his healing scalp. Without thinking, he'd used the Aveda Rosemary Mint shampoo Marla had provided in his shower and watched in horror as his plush brown #21 eddied down the drain. He never dreamed to pack his bronzer and his collection of the ever so subtle "Just for Him" eye makeup he'd purchased from the dermatologist who'd done his laser skin resurfacing. It wasn't as if he were a transvestite or anything, but a little skillfully applied makeup just enhanced his already considerable potential. It opened up his eyes, gave his face a little punch. So, on this morning, as he prepared to accuse his would-be assassin, the slayer of his beloved Barbie Lee, he had to appear in public with white plugs sprouting from an unbronzed scalp topping sparse wispy brows which defined rheumy close set lash-less eyes. All of his potential was home on his dresser zipped up in his alligator cosmetics case. If only he'd at least remembered his Alain Mikli glasses. He could hide behind those and cover a multitude of sins.

Trumpet strode directly to the front of the room, directly to Fuller and Acumulada. It was the first time Fuller had noticed the size of the man's hands. Little toddler hands, fingers holding fingers to keep them still, to keep them from building a little church with a steeple, open the door and see all the people.

"So, Officer," he got far too close to Fuller's nose as he spat this salutation. Fuller thought for a moment that it might be an interesting experiment to move back, inch by silent inch, in an effort to maintain the appropriate distance between his nose and Trumpet's unmascara-ed eyes. How long would it take for them to find that they had moved as one unit to the opposite side of the room? Not now. No time for fooling around. This was serious business. This was time for him to make an arrest and crack this case in front of everyone right here in Marla Stone's library. Right here before the Hammerston Police could get here and put him where they thought he belonged – answering phones and taking coffee orders.

"Good morning, Mr. Trumpet. Glad to see you could join us. Thank you."

"I'm glad you're grateful, young man." His little flickering fingers flew up to his face, but the right hand caught the left and he shoved both hands into his pockets. "At a time like this, a man should be able to be in seclusion, to be away from the prying eye of the public" he glanced around the room at the "*prying public*" to which he referred.

He continued, "As you can well imagine, I believe this matter should be left to the professionals, to people who know what they're doing. I don't believe the attempt on my life and my wife's unfortunate involvement in it should be treated as a parlor game for your amusement. But, because I am a generous man, I've agreed to this meeting to hear this information you claim to have. There are so many people in this house", he again threw his reptile glance around the library "who wish to do me harm. It's, it's quite frightening, really. I had no idea I had so many enemies. So many enemies right here in my new community. In the community my beloved wife and I had planned to make our new home. To think that there are so many of them," he scanned the room one more time. "You, who would wish me harm. Who would poison my food. Who would wish me dead."

He was beginning to break down. He took a deep breath; both hands flew momentarily from his pockets to create a stranglehold around his neck. He then forced them back to their confines. "I'm not sure why I even agreed to attend this morning. But, since I'm a man of my word, here I am."

Fuller squeezed Pam's hand and walked across the room to where Acumulada stood with Marla. An anticipatory buzz started with Florence and Everett and worked its way around the room.

Marla addressed the assemblage. "Ladies and Gentlemen, I know the events of this past evening have been shocking and disturbing to us all. I need you all to realize that we have resolution in this matter. Thanks to the brilliant police work of our own dear boy, Fuller Arden. Fuller will address us and fill us all in on the breakthroughs he's made in this case which he will then hand over to the Hammerston Police. Just as soon as our rescuer Bomatumbi arrives and realizes our predicament, the police will be notified and this unfortunate little episode will be behind us. It will be just a few short hours. In this case, though, we have much to be grateful for to darling Fuller, as will the police once they arrive. Their work will have been done for them. They will be handed an open and shut case." She beamed with pride and nodded to Fuller.

Fuller cleared his throat. "It's been quite a night and," he paused "quite a morning." I know you've all been talking amongst yourselves and many of you may have your own theory about what happened here last night. It was a terrible tragedy and we are very sorry for the unfortunate Mrs. Trumpet. As I'm sure you've heard, there are so many motives. It's hard to believe, really, that one man could have so many enemies, so many who were right here at the same dinner table with him last night. But, there it is."

Fuller walked to the board he had set up beside the fireplace. Marla had dozens in the house that she used for her classes. With the thoughts of her new TV career, she was hoping that this would be the last time she'd smell the smell of those extra broad permanent markers in her lovely library. Fuller flipped over the first sheet of paper revealing a list of names of dinner guests.

"For those of you who perhaps are just waking up and haven't had a chance to talk with your neighbors, here it is in a nutshell. Among the guests attending the dinner last night, we had", he pointed schoolmarm style to number one on his list, "Miss Noone who was mad as a hatter about her neon tubing being discontinued, neon tubing that was manufactured by Mr. Trumpet's company."

He moved down the list. "We had Everett Bainbridge who some might have thought was toying with the idea of trying to find a way to reacquire his minimally invasive surgical instruments company, the one he had sold to Trumpet."

Using the marker as a pointer, "We have Addie Coolidge who is a recent Native American convert and advocate for the plight of her people who found out that Mr. Trumpet had made a deal on some Indian land in New Jersey that had, shall we say, an overall negative impact on the indigenous peoples of New Jersey. Mrs. Franklin, I'm reluctant to say so in front of everyone, but you were talking as if you had it in for Mr. Trumpet as well. Even my own fiance, Pam", his eyes found Pam's across the room. "Even she was suspected by some because of the shoddy treatment her father received in the aborted acquisition of his emu ranch by Mr. Trumpet's company."

Trumpet was on his feet, "That's how business gets done in this country. Those people have no business wanting to *kill* me, for crissakes. That's just how business gets done." He glared at Addie Coolidge. "You brought me here last night for crissakes."

"Yes, Mr. Trumpet. I know how business gets done in this country. I have an MBA from Wheaton."

"Isn't that Wharton? The Wharton School?"

Fuller sneered. "No. Actually it's Wheaton. It's a combination MBA and early childhood education."

"So, to continue. All of these people may have had a motive to kill Jack Trumpet. But none of them did." Fuller hesitated. "That's not what I mean. You can see that Mr. Trumpet is not dead. He's still quite alive. What I mean is that none of those people tried to kill Mr. Trumpet and by accident poison Mrs. Trumpet." His voice was beginning to crack. "You know what I mean."

Acumulada leaned over and whispered in Fuller's ear, little hissed droplets of saliva escaping past her gold tooth.

Reinvigorated by her encouragement, Fuller went on. "Yes, as I was saying. We've all be focusing on a scenario where Mr. Trumpet is the intended victim. But, what if *Mrs.* Trumpet had been the intended victim?" A hush fell over the room. "Who then would be the most likely suspect?" The hush gave way to a murmur; the murmur to a gasp. Walter Coolidge shot Patrick his trademarked I-feel-your-pain beard nod. "Why Mrs. Marla Stone that's who. Who else would benefit from the death of Mrs. Trumpet? With Barbie Lee gone, the new TV show, the one that she had just signed on, would be the sole property of Marla Stone." A hush fell on the room. A hush except for the outburst coming from Jack Trumpet. "She's the killer. I told you. She did it. You must do your duty now and arrest that woman".

"But, we all know Marla couldn't have done it," Fuller went on, ignoring the multi colored man. "That substance she had at the table was nothing more than Chinese herbs for her headaches. Nothing more than that. And, she certainly wouldn't have spoiled her own gazpacho." He scanned the room, and saw for the first time looking back at him the look he'd worn in every classroom he'd ever sat in. For the first time in his life he felt the pain of the teachers who had been subjected to him as a student

'I believe you all know Miss, er, that is, Senorita Acumulada del rio Maria Candelario." Everyone nodded, bored and confused, longing for an end to this dreary story. "Senorita Candelario has been assisting me all morning. She is a very astute and clever woman. She's a very keen observer. Not only does she have above average physical senses, she's extremely good at intuiting a sub context."

No one was getting it. That dumb donkey hit in the head with a 2 x 4 look bombarded him once again. He made a mental note to personally apologize to every professor he'd ever had and have his family foundation increase their donation to Dartmouth College and, throw in a few bucks for the graduate school at Wheaton.

Acumulada handed Fuller a VHS tape and two small sealed ziplock bags. Jack Trumpet squinted. His Lasek corrected eyes were not quite up to the task of determining the bag's contents from his vantage point across the room.

Fuller was beginning to enjoy this. His initial stage fright had subsided; people, all the people were looking at him and he was going to get all the credit for this. This was a good thing. "Yes. We've been focusing on Mr. Trumpet as the intended victim and why? Why? Because that idea was planted in our heads. Planted in our heads by ...", he paused for what he hoped was effect. Lucretia Franklin was the first to get it.

"Jesus H. Christ. By him. By the husband. By Trumpet, by God. He did it. He did it. Of course." She turned her leathery face towards Dr. Franklin and glared. "Everyone knows you should always suspect the husband first".

"I was acquited. I didn't do shit."

Old Mr. Young raised his walking stick to the confused P.D. Quinn. Poor P.D. The effects of all those concussions on the gridiron were beginning show. "Not you, you jackass. Fuller's talking about Trumpet. He's talking about Trumpet."

Trumpet was horrified. "How dare you accuse me, you". He couldn't find the word. "I'm the bereaved, grieving husband. I'm a widower now. I'm a widower. Don't you understand. I'm alone in the world."

"Alone in the world with your wife's money. It was your wife who owned the controlling shares of stock in Conglomotron isn't that so?"

Acumulada reached into her apron and handed a copy of *BARON'S* to Fuller.

"She and I were always a team."

"It was, was it not, Mrs. Trumpet's father who started the company and structured it in such a way that the majority of the voting stock would remain in her hands for as long as she lived?" Fuller was euphoric. Fuller was beginning to think that he should try law school. "And, isn't it true that there could be no salary increases or bonuses paid without your wife's approval?" He was waiting for Hamilton Burger to object. "And, isn't it true that your extravagant lifestyle was beginning to stretch you a little too thin. All this conspicuous consumption was beginning to come out of your own pocket, a pocket that was not that deep. And, isn't it true, Mr. Trumpet, that your wife was planning to cut you off without a dime just as soon as her TV show, the one she was going to do with Marla, became a hit. Once she had an identity of her own, she could then afford to drop you."

"We were very much in love."

Fuller felt he had a real knack for this cross examination thing. He walked over to Lulu Noone and handed her the VHS tape he held in his hands.

"Miss Noone, do you know what this is?"

"A video tape?"

"No. No. Miss Noone. Do you know what's on this tape?"

Lulu adjusted the little square of cloth hidden amongst her curls.

"I can't see through this … it's a tape … I don't know … it's a tape … what do you think … I'm not able to see through black plastic. Some people think I can, but I can't. What do you think …?"

"Miss Noone. Lulu, do you remember what we talked about earlier. You and I and Miss Candelario."

"About the nannycam?" The pink of her cheeks was beginning to deepen.

"Yes, About the nannycam."

"I didn't put it up. It was Mr. Stone's idea. It was pretty flattering actually." She became coy. "To be guarded that way I mean." She smiled a tiny, contented smile thinking of the many kindnesses of her late patron.

Lucretia Franklin longed for a smoke. The nicotine patch she'd applied last night wore off a long time ago. "What the hell is this woman talking about? Can we get on with it? He did it. Let's just all agree and get out of here."

Beads of perspiration were starting on the fuzzy little mustache on Lulu Noone's upper lip.

Fuller prodded Lulu to go on. "What about the camera?"

"You say, I can't. You say. It's too embarrassing."

Fuller was the soul of composure.

"This is difficult for Miss Noone. She only learned about this today. And, she is quite modest about the value of her work. So, Miss Candelario and I will fill you in." Fuller gestured for Acumulada to join him. As you're all probably aware, there is nothing that goes on in this house or its immediate environs that Senorita Candelario is not aware of."

The blush that started on Acumulada's brown face seemed to engulf her entire squat little body. "Please, senor, please. Por favor."

"She has been invaluable to me during this investigation"

Jack Trumpet's fingers were playing high speed itsy bitsy spider lifting him up out of his seat. "This is not an investigation. You're not even a cop. This is a joke, a joke."

"Mr. Trumpet, I'm afraid I'm going to have to ask you to stay seated. I'd prefer not to have to use restraints".

He sat and he glared.

"Senorita Candelario ..."

She interrupted him "Acumulada, por favor, senor".

"Acumulada, of course. Apparently, when Mrs. Stone's late husband began purchasing Miss Noone's neon paintings and they were installed in the house, Mr. Stone, certain of the future investment value of the paintings", he nodded towards the not yet famous artist, "installed what they're calling now a nanny cam system. Mr. Stone's friend, Neon Jimmy installed a security system along with the paintings. Every room where a Noone painting hung was fitted with a motion activated hidden video camera. Someone walked into the room, the motion sensor activated the camera and it started rolling. It was a pretty sophisticated system. Each camera was independently operated and powered by a power cell. No electricity is needed for its operation. And, it was so carefully concealed, Mrs. Stone didn't even know about it. Miss Candelaria, er, Acumulada was the only one who was aware of the system. The whole party last night, every bit of it, was recorded. The camera is very sophisticated. It's digital, can record virtually forever. State of the art." He held up the tape he'd been playing with and placed it carefully in front of Jack Trumpet.

Dr. Franklin saw the gaping hole in Fuller's as yet unarticulated theory. He raised his hand to challenge the inexperienced teacher. "Fuller, the video system couldn't have worked during the dinner party. Once the power went out, the video system had to have gone out too."

Fuller was ready for this argument. "You're absolutely right, Dr. Franklin, as usual. Of course it was not functioning during the power outage. During the time it *was* recording during the party, when the power was still on, who knows what it was able to pick up what with all the milling around, sitting, standing, backs to the camera, obscured views. Probably just a jumble in a room full of people. But," he paused for emphasis "But, it did work during the toasts and *before* the party and during the preparations for the party. This system was not meant to record dinner parties. It was a security camera meant to electronically guard those paintings. One person walking around trying to remove the painting, that would be recorded. And, one person in an empty dining room moving and rearranging place cards on the table, that is what this system was able to record."

"Oh bloody hell, Fuller". Marla face went white. "You're brilliant! How did you figure this out?"

"Acumulada. She's the one. She suspected all along. She noticed immediately that the seating arrangement had been changed. She knew Marla would never seat a husband and wife together. So, when their cards turned up beside one another, she smelled a rat. And, when she smelled the bowl Mrs. Trumpet's gazpacho had been in, she smelled rat poison. So, after taking a look at the security video, this afternoon, she kept her very keen ears open all night and today. As I said, she's the only one who knew about the security camera. She saw footage of Mr. Trumpet here rearranging the placecards so that his wife would be seated in a seat with lighting most unflattering to her and ensure that she'd want to move. He then, would graciously offer to exchange seats with her."

Jack Trumpet needed no bronzer now. The morning's excitement had been enough of a jolt to flush anyone all the way down to the roots of his white plugs.

Fuller continued. "While he was seated at his originally assigned seat, he had ample opportunity to sprinkle the cyanide into the gazpacho which his wife would ultimately ingest."

Trumpet dismissed Fuller's theory with a shrug. "That's absurd."

Fuller was undaunted. He held aloft one of the ziplock bags, the one containing Barbie Lee Trumpet's place card. "Well, Mr. Trumpet, what about this card? Would you have any objection to us testing this card for your fingerprints or DNA or tissue samples?"

"Of course it would have my fingerprints on it. I touched it", he paused. "Probably two or three times last night. When I was helping to seat my wife, when I reached across the table to touch her face or hair as I frequently do, just out of love. I frequently just touched her face and gazed into her eyes. Of course it would have my fingerprints. You're going to have to do better than that."

"Well then, how about this?" he held up the video tape "This was found in his room this morning."

Trumpet nervously slurped up his latte. His flickering fingers juggled his coffee cup sending it soaring into the air, landing spilling, saturating the cassette. "Oh, my." Suddenly, he had the cassette, mopping, wiping, he flipped open the protective plastic. "Hey, look at this. This tape has been cut. And, now it's filled with coffee. There's no way we'll ever know what was on it. Will we? What a shame." He sat back, his fingers stilled and self-satisfied that he'd taken care of that little detail. "You're an amateur, Arden. You're playing a guessing game. But, you're playing with the big boys now." Trumpet was now taking the offensive. "I'll see your ass in court when I sue you for everything you and your family are worth for defamation of character, for libel. You'll be paying me off till you look like", he flipped his little white plugs in the direction of Old Mr. Young, "him." He grinned an evil smug sneer. "You know, you really should be more careful about what you say about people. You really shouldn't pay attention to these non-documented workers." He whispered, "They don't get it sometimes."

"Oh, I get it, Senor. I get it all right." Acumulada was dangerously close to Jack Trumpet's face.

"Come any closer and I'll see your skinny ass on the next boat back to whatever jungle it is you came from." He turned to the others in the library "You people have nothing. You're accusing me based on nothing. I did nothing wrong. I'm a grieving man. And you've got this savage harassing me. You can't expect me to behave appropriately. I'm not in my right mind right now. I'm a grieving man." He sobbed. "I don't know what's going on here. There's nothing on that tape that could possibly have implicated me. I don't know why it was in my room, it was planted I'm sure. I don't know what came over me. I'm just ... just in a ... state of shock, I guess."

"How about this, then?" Fuller waved the second ziplock bag. "These white crystals were found in the pocket of that very jacket you're wearing."

Trumpet instinctively shoved his hands into his pockets. The fingers did an exploratory sweep. Nothing.

"I clean the room, I tidy up, I pick up the clothes from the floor, and from under the bed is the tape. Mister, you sit there wanting the coffee and don't even put on the pants. You sit there with everything all hanging out everywhere. I think this guy wants the jacket pressed or something. Pressed all right. This is what is inside. This."

Dr. Franklin stood solemnly. "I'm afraid I concur, Mr. Trumpet. That substance is definitely cyanide. I have a test kit in my bag if you'd like confirmation. But I can almost certainly assure you, it's cyanide. Once the police get here, the jacket can be tested for the presence of cyanide as well."

Trumpet began to weep, silent tears at first, chin quivering. The emotions then progressed to all out sobbing, wailing. "You people. How can you be so hateful? What have I ever done to you? First my wife is brutally murdered and then you have the gall to accuse me?? Me?? No one loves my wife", he caught himself "loved my wife more than I did. And you accuse me of her murder. Then this woman plants this stuff in my room. A video tape, cyanide. It's probably cocaine. It's probably *her* cocaine smuggled in from *her* country. All this just because I had the audacity to want to join your club, just because I'm not from an old Yankee family like the rest of you, just because I had to work my way up to the top." He sneered. "You people should be ashamed of yourself".

The silence of several consciences being examined fell over the room. Lucretia felt terrible. The poor man. He had after all, been through enough already. She could identify with the unexpected death of a spouse, or in her case the unexpected survival of a spouse. Pam knew all too well the pain of losing a loved one and wanted to help Trumpet try to get through this. Noone knew first hand what it was like to be the victim of a conspiracy. Trying to explain to someone about the conspiracy was like being bound in Chinese handcuffs. The harder one tried to break free, the tighter and tighter the web around you became. She must try to help her fellow victim.

Fuller, Marla and Acumulada were steadfast.

Fuller was not letting his catch off the hook. "Ladies and gentlemen, once the electricity is turned back on and we can review the security camera, I think you will clearly see that Mr. Trumpet here tampered with the placecards, causing his wife to sit in unflattering light. A situation which he knew she would never tolerate. That, coupled with the cyanide found in his pocket and his admission that he knew his wife was poisoned with cyanide will easily convict him in a court of law."

"Arden", Trumpet hissed, "what are you talking about? That tape has been destroyed. It is unplayable. We all saw it. It was severed and then I inadvertently spilled hot coffee all over it. It's of no value whatsoever."

"I'm sorry, Mr. Trumpet. Did I say that cassette was from the security camera? I thought I made it clear that the security camera was digital. It records in a continuous loop. The tape you destroyed, the tape found under your bed, the tape you thought was from the security camera belongs to Miss Candelario."

"You made one big mistake, Trumpet that Acumulada picked up on."

"And what was that? Did I forget to bless myself before dinner?"

"You knew before anyone told you that your wife had been poisoned with cyanide. You said she hated any bitter taste. How would you have known it was cyanide unless it was you who put it in her soup?"

"That's ridiculous. Just a good guess. A stab in the dark."

"We, Acumulada and I allowed you to overhear us talking about the security camera. We left a tape on the sideboard near one of the paintings. It was sufficiently hidden so that you'd think it wasn't just left lying around. It didn't take you long to take the bait." Fuller walked over to Acumulada's side. "You wanted to say one more final goodbye to your wife in the dining room and requested privacy. Privacy to rifle through the room and find and destroy the tape and bring it back to your room".

The freshly examined consciences were once again ready to listen, ready to assign blame to Jack Trumpet.

"That was my tape you broke up, Mister," Acumulada said. "That's the show of Cassie's wedding to Prince Richard of San Cristobel."

"The Guiding Light", Fuller explained. "Miss Candelario watches *The Guiding Light* every day and when she can't watch, she tapes the episodes."

Trumpet was crestfallen. "So, the security camera?"

"You the star, mister. You movin' and you sprinklin'", Acumulada grinned.

The golden grin seemed to coincide with a rumble of the sump pumps from the basement and a flood of light pouring out of every room in the house.

The shrill whistle of the Coast Guard launch heralded their arrival. They had found them! Bomatumbi! Finally he was here.

Jack Trumpet slumped in his chair, defeated, clutching in his tiny hands episode number 9731.

The end

978-0-595-46981-9
0-595-46981-7

Printed in the United States
93859LV00006BB/103/A

9 780595 469819